Norman Macleod

**The Starling**

Vol. 2

Norman Macleod

**The Starling**
*Vol. 2*

ISBN/EAN: 9783337408800

Printed in Europe, USA, Canada, Australia, Japan

Cover: Foto ©Andreas Hilbeck / pixelio.de

More available books at **www.hansebooks.com**

# THE STARLING

## 𝔄 Scotch Story

### By NORMAN MACLEOD, D.D.

ONE OF HER MAJESTY'S CHAPLAINS

### VOL. II.

Anchora Spei

ALEXANDER STRAHAN, PUBLISHER

56, LUDGATE HILL, LONDON

1867

# CONTENTS OF VOLUME II.

# CONTENTS.

## CHAPTER VIII.

## CHAPTER IX.

## CHAPTER X.

## CHAPTER XI.

## CHAPTER XII.

## CHAPTER XIII.

## CHAPTER XIV.

## CHAPTER XV.

# CHAPTER I.

AS the evening drew on, the family who occupied the keeper's house gathered together like crows to their rookery. Mrs. Hugh, who had been helping at a large washing in "the big house," returned with a blythe face, full of cheer and womanly kindness.

"Hech! but I hae had sic a day o't! What a washing! an' it's no' half dune! But wha hae we here?" she asked, as she espied Jock seated near the fire. "Dae I ken ye?" she further inquired, looking at him with a sceptical smile,

VOL. II.                    B

as if she feared to appear rude to one whom she ought, perhaps, to have recognised.

Jock, with a sense of respect due to her, rose, and said, "I houp no', for maybe I wad be nae credit tae ye as an aqua'ntance."

"A freen' o' my cousin's, Adam Mercer, o' Drumsylie," remarked old Spence. "Sit doon, my man."

"I'm glad tae see ye," said the happy sonsy wife, stretching out her hand to Jock, who took it reluctantly, and gazed in the woman's face with an awkward expression.

"It's been saft weather, and bad for travellin', and ye hae come a far gait," she continued; and forthwith began to arrange her house. Almost at her heels the children arrived. There were two flaxen-haired girls, one ten and the other about twelve, with bare feet, and their locks tied up like sheaves of ripe golden grain.

Then came in a stout lad of about seven, from school and play. All looked as fresh and full of life as young roe from the forest.

"Gang awa, bairns, and snod yersels," said Mrs. Hugh.

"This man," said old Spence, who was jealous of his authority over the household, pointing to Jock, "wull tak' his supper wi' us. He's tae sleep in the stable-laft."

"He's welcome, he's welcome," said Mrs. Hugh. "The bed's nae braw, but it's clean, and it's our best for strangers."

The last to enter, as the sun was setting, was John, the eldest, a lad of about fourteen, the very picture of a pure-eyed, ruddy-complexioned, healthy, and happy lad. He had left school to assist his father in attending to his duties.

"What luck, Johnnie?" asked his father, as

the boy entered with his fishing basket over his shoulder.

" Middlin' only," replied John, " the water was raither laigh, and the tak' wasna guid. There were plenty o' rises, but the troots were unco' shy. But I hae gotten, for a' that, a guid wheen ; " and he unslung his basket and poured out from it a number of fine trout.

Jock's attention was now excited. Here was evidence of an art which he flattered himself he understood, and could speak about with some authority.

" Pretty fair," was his remark, as he rose and examined them ; " whaur got ye them ? "

" In the Blackcraig water," replied the boy.

" Let me luik at yer flee, laddie ? " asked Jock. The boy produced it. " Heckle, bad !—ye should hae tried a teal's feather on a day like this."

Johnnie looked with respect at the stranger. " Are *ye* a fisher ? " he asked.

" I hae tried my han'," said Jock. And so the conversation began, until soon the two were seated together at the window. Then followed such a talk on the mysteries of the craft as none but students of the angle could understand :—the arrangement and effect of various " dressings," of wings, bodies, heckles, &c., being discussed with intense interest; until all acknowledged Jock as a master.

" Ye seem tae understan' the business weel," remarked Hugh.

" I wad need," replied Jock. " Whan a man's life, no' to speak o' his pleasure, depen's on't, he needs tae fish wi' a watchfu' e'e and canny han'. But at a' times, toom or hungry, it's a great diverteesement ! "

Both Johnnie and his father cordially assented to the truth of the sentiment.

" Eh, man !" said Jock, thus encouraged to speak on a favourite topic, "what a conceit it is when ye reach a fine run on a warm spring mornin', the wuds hotchin' wi' birds, an' dauds o' licht noos and thans glintin' on the water ; an' the water itsel' in trim order, a wee doon, after a nicht's spate, and wi' a drap o' porter in't, an' rowin' and bubblin' ower the big stanes, curlin' into the linn and oot o't ; and you up tae the henches in a dark neuk whaur the fish canna see ye ; an' than to get a lang cast in the breeze that soughs in the bushes, an' see yer flee licht in the verra place ye want, quiet as a midge lichts on yer nose, or a bumbee on a flower o' clover, an'——"

Johnnie was bursting with almost as much excitement as Jock, but did not interrupt him except with a laugh expressive of his delight.

" An' than," continued Jock, " whan a muckle chiel o' a salmon, wi'oot time tae consider whether yer flee is for his wame or only for his mooth— whether it's made by natur' or by Jock Hall,— plays flap! and by mistak' gangs to digest what he has gotten for his breakfast, but suspec's he canna swallow the line alang wi' his mornin' meal till he taks some exercise!—an' then tae see the line ticht, and the rod bendin' like a heuk, and tae fin' something gaun frae the fish up the line and up the rod till it reaches yer verra heart, that gangs *pit pat* at yer throat like a tickin' watch; until the bonnie cratur', efter rinnin' up and doon like mad, noo skulkin' aside a stane tae cure his teethache, then bilkin' awa wi' a scunner at the line and trying every dodge, syne gies in, comes tae yer han' clean beat in fair play, and lies on the bank sayin' ' Wae's me ' wi' his tail, an' makin' his will wi' his gills and mooth time aboot !—eh, man ! it's splendid !" Jock wearied himself with the description.

" Whaur hae ye fished ?" asked Hugh, after a pause during which he had evidently enjoyed Jock's description.

" In the wast water and east water ; in the big linn an wee linn, in the Loch o' the Whinns, in the Red Burn, an' in——"

" I dinna ken thae waters at a'," remarked the keeper, interrupting him, "nor ever heard o' them !"

" Nor me," chimed in old John, " though I hae been here for mair than fifty year."

" Maybe no'," said Jock with a laugh," for they're in the back o' the beyonts, and that's a place few folk hae seen, I do assure you—ha ! ha ! ha !"

Jock had, in fact, fished the best streams watched by the keepers throughout the whole district. Young John was delighted with this new acquaintance, and looked up to him with the greatest reverence.

"What kin' o' flee duve ye fish wi'?" asked Johnnie. "Hae ye ony aboot ye e'enoo?"

"I hae a few," said Hall, as he unbuttoned his waistcoat, displaying a tattered shirt within, and diving into some hidden recess near his heart, drew forth a large old pocket-book and placed it on the table. He opened it with caution and circumspection, and spread out before the delighted Johnnie, and his no less interested father, entwined circles of gut, with flies innumerable.

"That's the ane," Jock would say, holding up a small, black, hairy thing, "I killed ten dizzen wi'—thumpers tae, three pun's some o' them—

afore twa o' clock. Eh, man, he's a murderin'
chiel this!" exhibiting another. "But it was this
ither ane," holding up one larger and more
gaudy, "that nicked four salmon in three hours
tae their great surprise! And thae flees," taking
up other favourites, "wi' the muir-fowl wing and
black body, are guid killers; but isna this a
cracker wi' the wee touch o' silver? it kilt mair
salmon—whaur, ye needna speer—than I could
carry hame on a heather wuddie! But, Johnnie,"
he added after a pause, "I maun, as yer freen',
warn ye that it's no' the flee, nor the water, nor
the rod, nor the win', nor the licht, can dae the
job, wi'oot the watchfu' e'e and steady han', an' a
feelin' for the business that's kin' o' born wi' a
fisher, but hoo that comes aboot I dinna ken—I
think I could maist catch fish in a boyne o' water
if there were ony tae catch!"

# CHAPTER II.

WHILE the preparations for supper were going on within doors, Jock went out to have a "dauner," or saunter, but, in truth, from a modest wish to appear as if not expecting to be asked to partake of supper with the family.

The table was spread with a white home-made linen cloth, and deep plates were put down, each with a horn spoon beside it. A large pot, containing potatoes which had been pared before they were placed on the fire, was now put on the floor, and fresh butter with some salt having been added to its contents, the whole was beat and mashed with a heavy wooden beetle worked by Hugh and his son—for the work required no small patience and labour—into a soft mass, forming an excellent dish of " champed potatoes," which, when served up with rich milk, is " a dainty dish to set before a king," even without the four-and-twenty blackbirds. Then followed a second course of " barley scones," and thick crisp oatmeal cakes, with fresh butter, cheese, and milk.

Before supper was served Jock Hall was missed, and Johnnie sent in search of him. After repeated shouts he found him wandering about the woods, but had the greatest difficulty in persuading him to join the family. Jock said " It wasna for him tae gang ben,"—" he had had eneuch tae eat in the afternoon,"—" he wad hae a bite efter hin," &c. But being at last persuaded to accept the pressing invitation, he entered, and without speaking a word seated himself in the place allotted to him.

" Tak' in yer chair, Maister Hall,"—Jock could hardly believe his ears !—" and mak' what supper ye can," said Mrs. Hugh. "We're plain kintra folk hereawa',"—an apology to Jock for their having nothing extra at supper to mark their respect for a friend of the Sergeant's ! What were his thoughts ? The character of an impostor seemed forced upon him when he most desired to be an honest man.

Then the old man reverently took off his " Kilmarnock cool," a coloured worsted night-cap, and said grace, thanking God for all his mercies, " of the least of which," he added, " we are unworthy." After supper Mrs. Hugh gave a long account of the labours of the day, and of the big washing, and

told how she had met Lady Mary, and Lady
Caroline, and Lord Bennock, and how they had
been talking to the children, and "speering for
faither and grandfaither."

A happy family was that assembled under the
keeper's roof. The youngest child, a boy, was
ever welcome on old John's knee, who never
seemed able to exhaust the pleasure he derived
from his grandson's prattle. His large watch,
which approached in size to a house clock, with
its large pewter seal, was an endless source of
amusement to the child; so also was the splendid
rabbit shadowed on the wall, with moving ears
and moving mouth, created by John's hands; and
his imitation of dogs, cats, and all other domestic
animals, in which he was an adept ;—nay, his very
crutches were turned to account to please the
boy, and much more to please himself. The elder

daughters clung round their mother in a group, frankly talking to her in mutual confidence and love. The boys enjoyed the same liberty with their father, and indulged unchecked in expressions of affection. All was freedom without rudeness, play without riot, because genuine heartfelt affection united all.

Jock did not join in the conversation, except when he was asked questions by Mrs. Hugh about Drumsylie, its shops and its people. On the whole he was shy and reserved. Any one who could have watched his eye and seen his heart would have discovered both busy in contemplating a picture of ordinary family life such as the poor outcast had never before beheld. But Jock still felt as if he was not in his right place—as if he would have been cast out into the darkness had his real character been known. His impressions of a kind of life he never dreamt of were still more deepened when, before going to bed, the large Bible was placed on the table, and Hugh, amidst the silence of the family, said, " We'll hae worship." The chapter for the evening happened to be the fifteenth of St. Luke. It was as if written expressly for Jock. Are such adaptations to human wants to be traced to mere chance? Surely He who can feed the wild beasts of the desert, or the sparrow amidst the waste of wintry snows, can give food to the hungry soul of a Prodigal Son, as yet ignorant of the food he needs, and of the Father who alone can supply it.

They did not ask Jock if he would remain for evening worship. " The stranger within the gate " was assumed to be, for the time, a member of the household. It was for him to renounce his recognised right, not for the family to question it. But Jock never even argued the point with himself. He listened with head bent down as if ashamed to hold it up, and following the example set to him by the family, knelt down— for the first time in his life—in prayer. Did he pray? Was it all a mere form? Was it by constraint, and not willingly? What his thoughts were on such an occasion, or whether they were gathered up in prayer to the living God, who can tell! But if the one thought even, for the first time, possessed him, that maybe there was a Person beyond the seen and temporal, to whom the world and man belonged, whose Name he could now associate with no evil but with all good, who possibly knew him and wished him to be good like Himself;— if there was even a glimmer in his soul, as he knelt down, that *he* might say as well as others, and along with

them, " Our Father which art in Heaven," then
was there cast into his heart, though he knew
it not, the germ of a new life which might yet
grow into a faith and love which would be life
eternal.

The prayer of Hugh the keeper was simple,
earnest, and direct, a real utterance from one
person to another—yet as from a man to God,
couched in his own homely dialect to Him whom
the people of every language and tongue can
worship.  The prayer was naturally suggested by
the chapter which was read.  He acknowledged
that all were as lost sheep ; as money lost in the
dust of earth; as miserable prodigals lost to their
Father and to themselves, and who were poor
and needy, feeding on husks, having no satisfaction, and finding no man to give unto them.
He prayed God to bring them all into the fold

of the Good Shepherd, who had given his life for the sheep, and to keep them in it; to gather them as the lost coins into the treasury of Him who was rich, yet who for our sakes became poor; he prayed God to help them all to say "I will arise, and go to my Father," in the assured hope that their Father would meet them afar off, and receive them with joy. After remembering the afflicted in body and mind, the orphan and widow, the outcast and stranger, he asked that God, who had mercy on themselves who deserved nothing, would make them also merciful to others; and he concluded with the Lord's Prayer.

Had any one seen poor Hall that night as he lay in the hay-loft, a clean blanket under him and more than one over him, they might have discovered in his open eyes, and heard in his half-muttered expressions, and noticed even from his wakeful tossings to and fro, a something stirring in his soul the nature or value of which he himself could not comprehend or fully estimate.

# CHAPTER III.

OLD John Spence was an early riser. He did not share Charles Lamb's fears of indulging in the ambition of rising with the sun. The latter part of the day was to him a period of repose, a *sicsta* of half-sleepy meditation, which not unfrequently passed into a deep-toned sleep in his arm-chair. In a lucid interval, during the evening of Jock's arrival, he had been considering how he might best help the Sergeant out of his difficulties. He had not for a moment accepted of Jock's policy suggesting his lordship's interference in the great Drumsylie case. With the

instinct of an old servant, he felt that such
presumption on his part was out of the question.
So he had informed Jock, bidding him not to
think of his lordship, who would not and could
not do anything in the matter. He assured him
at the same time that he would try what could
be done by himself to muzzle Smellie. Having
accordingly matured his plans, he was ready at
daybreak to execute them. He embraced therefore the first opportunity of taking Hugh into
a small closet, where the little business which
required writing was generally transacted, and
where a venerable *escritoire* stood, in whose
drawers and secret recesses were carefully de-
posited all papers relating to that department of
his lordship's estate over which John was chief.

The door having been carefully barred, the
old keeper seated in a arm-chair, and his son

Hugh at the *escritoire*, John said, "Get the pen and paper ready."

"A' richt," said Hugh, having mended his pen and tried it on his thumb-nail, looking at it carefully as he held it up in the light.

"Weel, then, begin! Write—'Sir;' no' 'Dear Sir,' but jist 'Sir.' Of coorse ye'll pit the direction 'To Mr. Peter Smellie.' Eh?—halt a wee— should I say Mr. or plain Peter? Jist mak' it plain Peter—say, 'To Peter Smellie.'"

"To Peter Smellie," echoed Hugh.

"John Spence, keeper—or raither John Spence, *senior* keeper—wishes tae tell ye that ye're a scoondrill."

After writing these words with the exception of the last, Hugh said, "Be canny, faither, or maybe he micht prosecute you."

" Let him try't!" replied John; " but let

scoondrill stan'. It's the verra pooder and shot o' my letter ; wi'oot that, it's a' tow and colfin."

"I'm no' sure, faither, if I can spell't," said Hugh, who did not like the more than doubtful expression, and put off the writing of it by asking, " Hoo, faither, d'ye spell scoondrill ? "

" What ither way but the auld way ? "

" But I never wrote it afore, for I hae had little to dae wi' ony o' the squad."

" Weel, I wad say—s, k, oo, n, d, r, i, l, l, or to that effec'. Keep in the *drill* whatever ye dae, for that's what I mean tae gie him ! "

Having written this very decided introduction, Hugh went on with his letter, which when completed ran as follows :—

" John Spence, Senior Keeper, Castle Bennock, to Peter Smellie, Draper, Drumsylie.

" You are a skoondrill, and you kno it ! But

nobody else knos it but my son and me and
Serjent Mercer. I wuss you to understan' that
he knos all about yon black business o' yours,
20 year back. This comes to let you kno that
unless you leve him alone, and don't molest him,
I will send you to Botany Bay, as you deserve.
Medle not with the Sergeant, or it wull be to
your cost. Attend to this hint. I wull have you
weel watched. You are in Mr. Mercer's power.
Bewar !

                "Your serv'.

                    "JOHN SPENCE."

"I houp," said John, as he had the letter read
over to him, "that will mak the whitrat leave aff
sookin' the Sergeant's throat ! If no', I'll worry
him like a brock, or hunt him like a fox aff the
kintra side. But no' a word o' this, mind ye,
tae ony leevin' cratur, mair especial tae yon

trampin' chiel. Gie Smellie a chance, bad as he is. Sae let the letter be sent aff this verra nicht wi' Sandy the Post. The sooner the better. The nesty taed that he is! Him to be preaching tae a man like Adam oot o' his clay hole!"

The letter was despatched that night by the post. It was not thought discreet to intrust Jock with the secret, or to let Adam Mercer know in the meantime anything about this counter-mine.

Breakfast being over, Hall proposed to return to Drumsylie. Before doing so he wished some positive assurance of obtaining aid in favour of the Sergeant from Spence. But all he could get out of the keeper was to "keep his mind easy—no' to fear—he wad look efter the Sergeant."

Old Spence would not, however, permit ol Jock's immediate departure, but invited him to remain a day or two "and rest himsel'." It was benevolently added, that "he could help Johnnie to fish at an odd hour, and to sort the dogs and horses in ordinar' hours." The fact was, old Spence did not wish Hall to return immediately to Drumsylie, until events there had time to be affected by his letter to Smellie. Jock was too glad of the opportunity afforded him of proving that he might be trusted to do whatever work he was fitted for, and that he was not "a lazy tramper" by choice.

As the week was drawing to an end, Jock made up his mind to return to his old haunts, for home he had none. He had also an undefined longing to see the Sergeant, and to know how it fared with him.

But when the day arrived for his departure, Hugh suggested that perhaps Jock would like to see the Castle ? It was not, he said, every day he would have such a chance of seeing so grand a place, and maybe he might even see his lordship !—at a distance. Besides, it would not take him far out of his road ; and Hugh would accompany him a part of the way home, as he had to visit a distant part of the estate in the discharge of his professional duties.

Jock's curiosity was excited by the thought of seeing the great house not as a beggar or a poacher, but under the genteel protection of a keeper and confidential servant, and when a live lord might be scanned from afar without fear.

When Jock came to bid farewell to old Spence, he approached him, bonnet in hand, with every token of respect. He said little but " Thank ye —thank ye, Mr. Spence, for yer guidness ; " and whispering, added, " I'm sorry if I offended ye.

But maybe ye could get a job for me if I canna fa' in wi' honest wark at Drumsylie? I'll break my back, or break my heart, tae please you or ony dacent man that 'ill help me to feed my body—it's no mickle buik—and to cover't—and little will keep the cauld oot, for my hide is weel tanned wi' win' and weather."

Spence looked with interest at the poor but earnest pleader at his elbow, and nodded encouragingly to him.

"Eh, man!" said Jock, "what a pity ye dinna snuff! I wad lee ye my auld snuff-box 'gin ye wad tak' it."

Spence smiled and thanked him—ay even shook hands with him!—an honour which went to Jock's heart; and Spence added, "My compliments to my cousin Adam, and tell him to stan' at ease and keep his pooder dry."

Mrs. Spence had prepared a good "rung" of bread and cheese, which she stuffed into Jock's pocket to support him in his journey.

"Awfu' guid o' ye—maist awfu'!" said Jock, as he eyed the honest woman pressing the food into its ragged receptacle.

Jock looked round, and asked for Johnnie. On being told that he was at the stables, he went off to find him, and, having succeeded, took him aside and said—"Johnnie, laddie, I hae been treated by yer folk like a lord, tho' efter a' I dinna weel ken hoo a lord is treated; but, howsomdever, wi'oot ony clavers aboot it, here's a present for you o' the best buik o' flees in the haill kintra side. Tak' them, and welcome." And Jock produced his "Book of Sports," which had been his most cheerful companion for many a year, and almost forcing John to take it, added

" I hae a obligation to ax : never tell yer folk aboot it till I'm awa', and never tell ony stranger atween this and Drumsylie that ye got it frae Jock Ha'." And before the astonished boy could thank him as the generous giver of so many keys to unlock every pool of its treasures, on every day in the year and at all seasons, Jock ran off to join Hugh.

# CHAPTER IV.

IN a short time Hugh was conducting Jock towards the Castle. After they passed the lodge, and were walking along the beautiful avenue and beneath the fine old trees, with the splendid park sweeping around, and the turrets of the Castle in sight, Hugh said, "Now, Hall, dinna speak to onybody unless they speak to you, and gie a discreet answer. Dae my biddin'; for I'm takin' a great responsibility in bringin' ye in here. His lordship maybe wadna be pleased to see a trampin' chiel like you here. But I'll tak' care he doesna see ye, nor if possible hear tell o' ye."

"Never fear me," said Jock; "I'll be as quaet as a dead rabbit. But, Hugh man, I hae seen his lordship afore."

"Whaur?" asked Hugh, with an expression of astonishment.

"He ance tried me, as a maugistrat'," replied Jock, equally placid.

"Tried ye!" exclaimed Hugh, pausing in his walk as if he had got into one scrape and was about to enter a second—"tried ye for what?"

"Oh, never heed," said Jock; "dinna be ower particular. It was a job that ended in a drucken habble I got into wi' twa tailor chappies that struck me, and my head and e'e were bun' wi' a bluidy napkin at the trial, and his lordship wull no' mind on me; tho' faix! I mind on him, for he sent me tae jail."

"Was that a'?" carelessly remarked Hugh.

'Ye micht hae thrashed nine tailors and no'
got yersel' hurt; I gripped three o' them mysel'
when poachin'."

But Jock did not tell the whole history of one
of his own poaching affrays along with the tailors.

Hugh ensconced Jock in the shrubbery until
he ascertained from one of the servants that his
lordship had gone out to walk in the grounds,
that the ladies were taking an airing in the
carriage, and that it was quite possible to get
a peep into the great hall and the public rooms
opening from it, without being discovered. As
Hugh, accompanied by Jock, crept almost noiselessly along the passages, he directed with under-
breath Jock's attention to the noble apartments,
the arms and suits of mail hung round the wall
of the great entrance-hall, the stags' heads, the
stuffed birds, and one or two fine paintings of

boar-hunts. But when the drawing-room door was opened, and there flashed upon Jock's eyes all the splendour of colour reflected from large mirrors, in which he saw, for the first time, his own odd figure from crown to toe, making him start back as if he had seen a ghost, and when through the windows he beheld all the beauty of flowers that filled the parterres, dotted with *jets d'eaux*, white statues and urns, and sur- rounded by bowery foliage, a vision presented itself which was as new to him as if he had passed into Eden from the lodgings of Mrs. Craigie.

He did not speak a word, but only remarked it was " nae doubt unco braw, and wad hae cost a heap o' siller." But, as they were retreating, suddenly the inner door of the hall opened, and his lordship stood before them!

" Heeven be aboot us!" ejaculated Spence, and

in a lower voice added, "Dune for,—dune for
life!" He looked around him, as if for some means
of concealing himself, but in vain. The door by
which they had entered was closed. There was no
mode of exit. Jock, seeing only a plain-looking
little gentleman in a Glengarry bonnet and tweed
suit, never imagined that this could be a lord, and
was accordingly quite composed. Spence, with
his eyes fixed on the ground and his face flushed
to the roots of his hair, seemed speechless.

His lordship was a slight-built man, of about
forty, with pleasing hazel eyes and large moustache.
He had retired from the army, and was much
liked for his frank manner and good humour.
Seeing his keeper in such perplexity, accompanied
by so disreputable-looking a person, he said,
"Hollo, Spence! whom have you got here? I
hope not a poacher, eh?"

" I humbly beg your lordship's pardon; but, my lord, the fac' is——" stammered Hugh.

" Is that his lordship?" whispered Jock.

" Haud yer tongue!" replied Hugh in an undertone of intense vehemence. Then addressing his lordship, he said, " He's no poacher, my lord; no, no, but only——"

" Oh! an acquaintance, I suppose."

" No' that either, no' that either," interrupted Hugh, as his dignity was frying on account of his companion, whom he wished a hundred miles away, " but an acqua'ntance o' an acqua'ntance o' my faither's lang syne—a maist respectable man —Sergeant Mercer, in Drumsylie, and I took the leeberty, thinking yer lordship was oot, to——"

" To show him the house. Quite right, Spence; quite right; glad you did so." Then addressing Jock, he said, " Never here before, I suppose?"

Jock drew himself up, placed his hands along his sides, heels in, toes out, and gave the military salute.

" Been in the army ?   In what regiment ?   Have you seen service ?"

" Yes, sir—yes, my lord," replied Jock; " as yer honour says, I ha'e seen service."

This was information to Spence, who breathed more freely on hearing such unexpected evidence of Jock's respectability.

" Where ?" inquired his lordship, seating himself on one of the lobby chairs, and folding his arms.

" In the berrick-yaird o' Stirlin', yer honour, replied Jock; " but in what regiment I dinna mind.  It was a first, second, or third something or anither; but I hae clean forgotten the name and number."

" The barrack-yard?" said his lordship, laughing; " pray how long did you serve his Majesty
in that severe campaign."

" Aboot a fortnicht," said Jock.

" What!" exclaimed his lordship; " a fortnight
only?   And what after that?"

" I ran aff as fast as I could," said Jock;
" and never ran faster a' my days, till I reached
Drumsylie."

Hugh turned his back as if also to run away,
with sundry half-muttered exclamations of horror
and alarm.   His lordship burst into a fit of
laughter, and said,—" On my honour, you're a
candid fellow!"   But he evidently assumed that
Jock was probably a half-witted character, who
did not comprehend the full meaning of his
admission.   He was confirmed in his supposition
by Jock going on to give a history of his

military life in the most easy and simple fashion,—

"I listed when I was fou'; and though I had nae objections at ony time to fire a gun at a bird or a Frenchman, or tae fecht them that wad fecht me, yet the sodjers at Stirlin' made a fule o' me, and keepit me walkin' and trampin' back and forrid for twa weeks in the yaird, as if they were breakin' a horse; and I could dae naething, neither fish, nor e'en shoot craws, wi'oot the leave o' an ill-tongued corporal. I couldna thole that, could I? It wasna in the bargain, and sae I left, and they didna think it worth their while to speer after me."

"Egad!" said his lordship, laughing, "I dare say not, I dare say not! Do you know what they might have done to you if they had caught you, my man?" asked his lordship.

" Shot me, I expec'," said Jock; " but I wasna worth the pooder; and, tae tell the truth, I wad raither be shot like a gled for harryin' a paitrick's nest, than be kept a' my days like a gowk in a cage o' a berricks at Stirlin'! But I didna heed atweel whether they shot me or no'," added Jock, looking round him, and stroking his chin as if in a half dream.

" The black dog tak' ye!" said Spence, who lost his temper. " My lord, I declare——"

" Never mind, Spence, never mind; let him speak to me; and go you to the servants' hall until I send for you."

Spence bowed and retired, thankful to be released from his present agony. His lordship, who had a passion for characters which the keeper could not comprehend, gave a sign to Jock to remain, and then went on with the following catechism.

" What did your parents do ? "

" Little guid and mickle ill."

" Were you at school ? "

" No' that I mind o'."

" How have you lived ? "

" Guid kens ! "

" What have you been ? "

" A ne'er-do-weel—a kin' o' cheat-the-widdie. Sae folk tell me, and I suppose they're richt."

" Are you married ? "

" That's no' a bad ane, efter a' ! " said Jock, with a quiet laugh, turning his head away.

" A bad what ? " asked his lordship, perplexed by the reply.

" I jist thocht," said Jock, "yer honour was jokin', to think that ony wumman wad marry me! He ! he ! Lassies wad be cheaper than cast-awa shoon afore ony o' them wad tak Jock Ha'—

unless," he added, in a lower tone, with a laugh, " ane like Luckie Craigie. But yer lordship 'ill no' ken her, I'se warrant ?"

" I have not that honour," said his lordship, with a smile. " But I must admit that you don't give yourself a good character, anyhow."

" I hae nane to gie," said Jock, with the same impassible look.

" On my word," added his lordship, " I think you're honest !"

" It's mair," said Jock, " than onybody else thinks. But if I had wark, I'm no' sure but I wad be honest."

His lordship said nothing, but stared at Hall as if measuring him from head to foot. Jock returned his gaze. It was as if two different portions of a broken-up world had met. His lordship felt uncertain whether to deal with Jock

as a fool or as a reprobate. He still inclined to
the opinion that he had " a want," and accordingly continued his catechism, asking,—

" What would you like to have ? "

" It's no' for me tae say," replied Jock; " beggars
shouldna be choosers."

" Perhaps you would have no objection to have
this fine house—eh? " asked his lordship, with a
smile.

" I'll no' say that I wad," replied Jock.

" And what would you make of it ?"

" I wad," replied Jock, " fill't fu' wi' puir
ne'er-do-weel faitherless and mitherless bairns,
and pit Sergeant Mercer and his wife ower them
—that's Mr. Spence's cousin, ye ken."

" Hillo !" said his lordship, " that would make
a large party ! And what would you do with them,
when here assembled, my man ?"

" I wad feed them," said Jock, " wi' the sheep and nowt in the park, and the birds frae the heather, and the fish frae the burns, and gie them the flowers aboot the doors—and schule them weel, and learn them trades: and shoot them or hang them, if they didna dae weel efter hin."

" Ha! ha! ha! And what would you do with me and my wife and daughters?" asked his lordship.

" I wad mak you their faither, and them their mither and sisters. Ye never wad be idle or want pleasure, yer honour, among sic a hantle o' fine lads and lasses."

" Never idle—never idle! I should think not! But as to the pleasure! Ha! ha! ha!" And his lordship laughed with much glee at the idea of his being master of such an establishment.

" Eh! sir," said Jock, with fire in his eyes,

"*ye* dinna ken what poverty is! Ye never lay trimblin' on a stair-head on a snawy nicht; nor got a spoonfu' or twa o' cauld parritch in the mornin' tae cool ye, wi' curses and kicks tae warm ye, for no' stealin' yer ain meat; nor see'd yer wee brithers an' sisters deein' like troots, openin' their mooths wi' naethin' to pit in them; or faix ye wad be thankfu' tae help mitherless and faitherless bairns, and instead o' sendin' young craturs like them tae the jail, ye wad sen' aulder folk that ill-used and neglected them; ay, and maybe some rich folk, and some ministers and elders as weel, for helpin' naebody but themsel's!"

His lordship looked in silence with wide-open eyes at Jock; and for a moment, amidst his ease and luxury, his fits of *ennui* and difficulty in killing time, his sense of the shallowness and emptiness of much of his life, with the selfishness of idle society, there flashed upon his naturally kind heart a gleam of noble duties yet to perform, and noble privileges yet to enjoy, though not perhaps in the exact form suggested by Jock Hall. But this was not the time to discuss these. So he only said, " You are not a bad fellow—not at all. Wiser men have said more foolish things," he added, as if thinking to himself; and then approaching Jock with a kindly smile, offered him some money.

" Na! na!" said Jock, " I didna come here to beg ; I'll no' tak' onything."

" Come! come !" said his lordship, " you won't disoblige me, will you ?" and he thrust the money into Jock's hand; and ringing a bell, he ordered the servant who appeared in reply to it to take him to the servants' hall, and to send Hugh Spence to the business room.

Jock made a low bow and salaam, and retired.

" William," said his lordship to another servant, who happened to be passing, " go to the old clothes press, and select a complete suit for that poor fellow. Be kind to him: see that he has some food and a glass of beer."

When Hugh was summoned into the presence of his lordship, he had sad misgivings as to the object of the interview, and had carefully prepared a long apologetic speech, which however he had hardly begun when he was cut short by his lordship saying, " You have picked up a rare character, Spence, upon my honour! But I like the fellow. He is an original, and has something good in him. I can't quite make him out."

" Nor me either, my lord, I do assure you," interrupted Spence.

" But I have taken rather a fancy to him,"

continued his lordship. " He is neither knave nor fool; but seems to have been ill-used, and to have had a hard time of it. There is something about him which takes me, and if any friend of your father's has an interest in him, I won't object— quite the reverse—to your getting him something to do about the kennels. I really would like it. So look to him."

Hugh having made a low bow and remained discreetly silent, according to his own prudential aphorism of " least said being soonest mended," his lordship conversed on some business matters connected with the game, with which we have nothing to do, and then dismissed him.

# CHAPTER V.

WHEN Jock and Spence returned along the avenue, not a word was spoken for some time. Jock carried a large bundle, with the general contents of which both were acquainted. After awhile Spence remarked, as if to break the silence, " Weel, what do ye think o' his lordship ?"

" He looks a fine bit decent 'sponsible bodie," said Jock, as if speaking of a nobody.

" I should think sae !" remarked Hugh, evidently chagrined by the cool criticism of his companion.

" Were ye no' frighted for him ?" asked Hugh.

"Wha?—me?" replied Jock. "Frichted for what? He said naethin' tae fricht me. Certes, I was mair frichted when I stood afore him for threshin' the tailors! The man didna molest me, but was unco ceevil, as I was tae him, and he gied me siller and claes as I never got frae mortal man afore, no' tae speak o' a lord. Frichted! I was ower prood to be frichted."

"Aweel, aweel," said the keeper, "ye're a queer cratur, Jock! and if ye haena' gowd ye hae brass. I was trimblin' for ye!"

"Nae wunner," said Jock; "*ye* had somethin' tae lose, but I had naethin'. What could he dae to me but pit me oot o' the hoose? and I was gaun oot mysel'. Jock Ha' is ower far doon for ony mortal man tae pit him doon farther. He *may* be better, but he canna be waur. Naebody can hurt a dead doug, can they?"

"Tuts, Jock, my puir fallow," said Hugh, "I didna mean to flyte on ye. I ax yer pardon."

"Gae awa, gae awa wi yer nonsense, Mr. Spence!" replied Jock — "that's what naebody ever did, to ax my pardon, and it's no' for a man like you tae begin. Ye micht as weel ax a rattan's pardon for eatin' a' yer cheese! In troth I'm no gi'en mysel tae that fashion o' axin' pardons, for it wad be a heap o' trouble for folk to grant them. But, man, if I got wark, I would maybe be able to ax pardon o' a decent man, and tae get it tae for the axin'!"

"I'll no' forget ye, I do assure ye," said Spence, kindly. "You and me if I'm no' mista'en 'ill meet afore lang up the way at the cottage. His lordship is willin' tae gie ye wark, and sae am I and my faither."

Jock could not resist the new emotion which

prompted him to seize the keeper's hand and give it a hearty squeeze. On the strength of the renewed friendship, he offered him a snuff.

The keeper, from commands received from his lordship, found that he could not accompany Jock as far on his road as he had anticipated, but was obliged to part with him where his path to Drumsylie led across the moorland. Here they sat down on a heathery hill, when Spence said, "Afore we part, I wad like tae ken frae yersel', Jock, hoo *ye* are a freen' tae Adam Mercer?"

"I never said I was a freen' tae Adam Mercer," replied Jock.

Hugh, as if for the first time suspecting Hall of deception, said firmly, "But ye did that! I declare ye did, and my faither believed ye!"

"I never did sic a thing!" said Jock, as firmly, in reply. "For I couldna do't wi'oot a lee, and *that* I never telt tae you or yours, although in my day I hae telt ither folk an unco' heap tae ser' my turn. What I said was that Adam Mercer was a freen' tae me."

Hugh, not quite perceiving the difference yet, asked, " Hoo was he a freen' tae you ? "

" I'll tell ye," said Jock, looking earnestly at Hugh. " Had a man ta'en ye into his hoose, and fed ye whan stervin', and pit shoon on ye whan barefitted, and spak to ye, no' as if ye war a brute beast, and whan naebody on yirth ever did this but himsel', I tak it ye wad understan' what a freen' was ! Mind ye, that I'm no sic a gomeril —bad as I am—or sae wantin' in decency as to even tae mysel' to be the Sergeant's freen' ; but as I said, and wull say till I dee, he was *my* freen' ! "

" What way war ye brocht up that ye cam to be sae puir as to need Adam's assistance or ony ither man's? Ye surely had as guid a chance as ony o' yer neebors?"

Jock's countenance began to assume that excited expression which the vivid recollection of his past life, especially of his youth, seemed always to produce. But he now tried to check himself, when the symptoms of his hysteria began to manifest themselves in the muscles of his throat, by rising and taking a few paces to and fro on the heather, as if resolved to regain his self-possession, and not to leave his newly-acquired friend the keeper under the impression that he was either desperately wicked or incurably insane. A new motive had come into play—a portion of his heart which had lain, as it were, dormant until stimulated by the Sergeant's kindness, had assumed a power which was rapidly, under benign influences, gaining the ascendancy. In spite of, or rather perhaps because of, his inward struggle, his face for a moment became deadly pale. His hands were clenched. He seemed as if discharging from every muscle a stream of suddenly-generated electricity. Turning at length to Hugh, he said, with knit brow and keenly-piercing eyes, " What made ye ax me sic a question, Mr. Spence ?—What for ? I'll no' tell ye, for I canna tell you or ony man hoo I was brocht up ! "

But he did tell him—as if forced to do so in order to get rid of the demon—much of what our readers already know of those sad days of misery. "And noo," he added, " had ye been like a wild fox and the hoonds after ye, or nae mair cared for than a dowg wi' a kettle at its tail, hidin' half mad up a close ayont a midden ; or a cat nigh staned to death, pechin' its life awa' in a hole ; and if ye kent never a man or woman but wha hated ye, and if ye hated them ; and, waur than a', if ye heard your ain faither and mither cursing ye frae the time ye war a bairn till they gaed awa' in their coffins, wi' your curses followin' after them,—ye wad ken what it was to hae ae freend on yirth;— and noo I hae mair than ane!" And poor Jock, for the first time probably in his life, sobbed like a child.

Spence said nothing but "Puir fellow!" and whiffed his pipe, which he had just lighted, with more than usual vehemence.

Jock soon resumed his usual calm,

> " As one whose brain demoniac frenzy fires
> Owes to his fit, in which his soul hath tost,
> Profounder quiet, when the fit retires,—
> Even so the dire phantasma which had crost
> His sense, in sudden vacancy quite lost,
> Left his mind still as a deep evening stream."

The keeper, hardly knowing what to say, re-marked, " It's ae consolation, that your wicked faither and mither will be weel punished noo for a' their sins. *Ye* needna curse them! They're beyond ony hairm that ye can do them. They're cursed eneuch, I'se warrant, wi'oot your meddlin' wi' them."

"Guid forbid!" exclaimed Jock. "I houp no'! I houp no'! That wad be maist awfu'!"

"Maybe," said the keeper; "but it's what they deserve frae the han' o' justice. And surely when their ain bairn curses them, *he* can say naethin' against it."

"*I* never cursed them, did I?" asked Jock, as if stupified.

"Ye did that, and nae mistak'!" replied the keeper.

"Losh, it was a bad job if I did!" said Jock. "I'm sure I dinna want to hairm them, puir bodies, though they hairmed me. In fac'," he added, after a short pause, during which he kicked the heather vehemently, "I'm willin' tae let by-ganes be byganes wi' them, and sae maybe their Maker will no' be ower sair on them. Ye dinna think, Mr. Spence, that it's possible my faither and mither are baith in the bad place?"

"Whaur else wad they be, if no' there?" asked the keeper.

"It's mair than I can say!" replied Jock, as if in a dream. "I only thocht they were dead in the kirkyard. But—but—ken ye ony road o' gettin' them oot if they're yonner — burnin' ye ken?"

"Ye had better," said Hugh, "gie ower botherin' yersel' to take *them* oot; rather try, man, to keep yersel' oot."

"But I canna help botherin' mysel' aboot my

ain folk," replied Jock; "an' maybe they warna sae bad as I mak' them. I've seen them baith greetin' and cryin' tae God for mercy even whan they war fou; an' they aince telt me, after an awfu' thrashin' they gied me, that I wasna for my life tae drink or swear like them. Surely that was guid, Mr. Spence? God forgie them! God forgie them!" murmured Jock, covering his face with his hands; " lost sheep!—lost money!—lost, ne'er-do-weels! an' I'm here and them there! Hoo comes that aboot?" he asked, in a dreamy mood.

"God's mercy!" answered Hugh; "and we should be merciful tae ither folk, as God is mercifu' to oorsel's."

"That's what I wish thae puir sowls to get oot o' that awfu' jail for! But I'll never curse faither or mither mair," said Jock. "I'll sweer," he added, rising up, muttering the rhyme as solemnly as if before a magistrate:

> " If I lee, let death
> Cut my breath!"

"Dinna fash yersel' ower muckle," said the keeper, "for them that's awa. The Bible says, 'Shall not the Judge o' a' the yirth dae richt?' I wad think sae! Let us tak' care o' oorsel's, and o' them that's leevin', an' God will do what's richt tae them that's ayont the grave. He has mair wisdom and love than us!"

Jock was engaged outwardly in tearing bits of heather, and twisting them mechanically together; but what his inward work was we know not. At last he said, "I haena heard an aith sin' I left Drumsylie, and that's extraordinar' to me, I can assure you, Mr. Spence!"

The keeper, who, unconsciously, was calmly

enjoying the contemplation of his own righteousness, observed that " the kintra was a hantle
decenter than the toon." But in a better and
more kindly spirit he said to Jock, " I'll
stan' yer friend, Hall, especially sin' his lordship wishes me to help you. Ye hae got guid
claes in that bundle, I'se warrant — the verra
claes, mark ye, that were on himsel' ! Pit
them on, and jist think *what's* on ye, and be
dacent! Drop a' drinkin', swearin', and sic trash ;
bend yer back tae yer burden, ca' yer han' tae
yer wark, pay yer way, and keep a ceevil tongue
in yer head, and then ' whistle ower the lave o't !'
There's my han' to ye. Fareweel, and ye'll hear
frae me some day soon, whan I get a place ready
for ye aboot mysel' and the dougs."

" God's blessin' be wi' ye !" replied poor Jock.

They then rose and parted. Each after awhile

looked over his shoulder and waved his hand.

Jock ran back to the keeper when at some distance from him, as if he had lost something.

" What's wrang ?" asked Spence.

" A's richt noo !" replied Jock, as again he raised his hand and repeated his parting words. " God's blessin' be wi' ye ;" and then ran off as if pursued, until concealed by rising ground from the gaze of the keeper, who watched him while in sight, lost in his own meditations.

One of the first things Jock did after thus parting with Hugh was to undo his parcel, and when he did so there was spread before his wondering eyes such a display of clothing of every kind as he had never dreamt of in connexion with his own person. All seemed to his eyes as if fresh from the tailor's hands. Jock looked at his treasures in detail, held them up, turned them over, laid them down, and repeated the process with such a grin on his face and exclamations on his lips as can neither be described nor repeated. After awhile his resolution seemed to be taken : for descending to a clear mountain stream, he stripped himself of his usual habiliments, and, though they were old familiar friends, he cast them aside as if in scorn, stuffing them into a hole in the bank. After performing long and careful ablutions, he decked himself in his new rig, and tying up in a bundle his superfluous trappings, emerged on the moorland in appearance and in dignity the very lord of the manor !  " Faix," thought Jock, as he paced along, "the Sterlin' wasna far wrang when it telt me that 'a man's a man for a' that!'"

Instead of pursuing his way direct to Drumsylie, he diverged to a village half-way between Castle

Bennock and his final destination. With his money in his pocket, he put up like a gentleman at a superior lodging-house, where he was received with the respect becoming his appearance. Early in the morning, when few were awake, he entered Drumsylie, with a sheepish feeling and such fear of attracting the attention of its *gamins* as made him run quickly to the house of an old widow, where he hoped to avoid all impertinent inquiries until he could determine upon his future proceedings. These were materially affected by the information which in due time he received, that Adam Mercer had been suddenly seized with illness on the day after he had left Drumsylie, and was now confined to bed.

# CHAPTER VI.

IT was true, as Jock Hall had heard, that Sergeant Mercer was very unwell. The events of the few previous weeks, however trivial in the estimation of the great world, had been to him very real and afflicting. The ecclesiastical trials and the social annoyances, with the secret worry and anxiety which they had occasioned, began to affect his health. He grew dull in spirits, suffered from a sense of oppression, and was "head-achy," "fushionless," and "dowie." He resolved to be cheerful, and do his work; but he neither could be the one nor do the other. His wife prescribed for him out of her traditional pharmacopœia, but in vain. Then, as a last resort, "keeping a day in bed" was advised, and this was at once acceded to.

At the risk of breaking the thread of our narrative, or—to borrow an illustration more worthy of the nineteenth century—of running along a side rail to return shortly to the main line, we may here state, that at the beginning of the Sergeant's illness, a person, dressed in rather decayed black clothes, with a yellowish white neckcloth, looking like a deposed clergyman, gently tapped at his door. The door was opened by Katie. The stranger raised his broad-brimmed hat, and saluted her with a low respectful bow. He entered with head uncovered, muttering many apologies with many smiles. His complexion was dark; his black hair was smoothly combed back from his receding forehead, and again drawn forward in the form of a curl under each large ear, thus directing attention to his pronounced nostrils and lips; while his black eyes were bent down, as if contemplating his shining teeth. His figure was obese; his age between forty and fifty.

This distinguished-looking visitor introduced himself as Dr. Mair, and inquired in the kindest, blandest, and most confidential manner as to the health of "the worthy Sergeant," as he condescendingly called him. Katie was puzzled, yet pleased, with the appearance of the unknown doctor, who explained that he was a stranger— his residence being ordinarily in London, except when travelling on professional business, as on the present occasion. He said that he had devoted all his time and talents to the study of the complaint under which the Sergeant, judging

from what he had heard, was evidently labouring ;
and that he esteemed it to be the highest honour
—a gift from Heaven, indeed — to be able to
remedy it. His father, he stated, had been a
great medical man in the West Indies, and
had consecrated his life to the cure of disease,
having made a wonderful collection of medicines
from old Negroes, who, it was well known,
had a great knowledge of herbs. These secrets
of Nature his father had entrusted to him,
and to him alone, on the express condition
that he would minister them in love only. He
therefore made no charge, except for the medicine itself—a mere trifle to cover the expense
of getting it from the West Indies. Might he
have the privilege of seeing the Sergeant? One
great blessing of his medicines was, that if they
did no good—which rarely happened—they did

no harm. But all depended—he added, looking up towards heaven—on *His* blessing!

After a long unctuous discourse of this kind, accompanied by a low whine and many gestures expressive of, or intended to express, all the Christian graces, added to Nature's gifts, the doctor drew breath.

Katie was much impressed by this self-sacrificing philanthropist, and expressed a cordial wish that he should see the Sergeant. Adam, after some conversation with his wife, saw it was best, for peace sake, to permit the entrance of the doctor. After he had repeated some of his former statements and given assurances of his skill, the Sergeant asked him: "Hoo do I ken ye're speakin' the truth, and no' cheatin' me?"

"You have my word of honour, Sergeant!"

replied Dr. Mair, "and you don't think *I* would lie to you? Look at me! I cannot have any possible motive for making you unwell. Horrible thought! I hope I feel my sense of responsibility too much for that!" Whereupon he looked up to heaven, and then down into a black bag, out of which he took several phials and boxes of pills, arranging them on a small table at the window. He proceeded to describe their wonderful qualities in a style which he intended for the language of a scholarly gentleman, interlarding his speech with Latinized terms, to give it a more learned colouring.

"This medicine," he said, "acts on the spirits. It is called the *spiritum cheerabilum.* It cures depression; removes all nervous, agitating feelings —what we term *depressiones;* soothing the anxious mind because acting on the vital nerves—going to the root of every painful feeling, through the gastric juice, heart, and liver, along the spinal cord, and thence to the head and brain. This view is according to common-sense, you must admit. A few doses of such a medicine would put you on your legs, Sergeant, in a week! I never once knew it fail when taken perseveringly and with faith—with faith!" he added, with a benignant smile; "for faith, I am solemnly persuaded, can even yet remove mountains!"

"Doctor, or whatever ye are," said the Sergeant, in an impatient tone of voice, "I want nane o' yer pills or drugs; I hae a guid eneuch doctor o' my ain."

"Ha!" said Dr. Mair; "a regular practitioner, I presume? Yes, I understand. Hem! College bred, and all that."

"Just so," said the Sergeant. "Edicated,

as it were, for his wark, and no' a doctor by guess."

"But can you believe his word?" blandly asked Dr. Mair.

"As muckle, surely, as yours," replied the Sergeant; "mair especial' as guid and learned men o' experience agree wi' him, but no' wi' you."

"How do *you* know they are good and learned?" asked Dr. Mair, smiling.

"Mair onyhoo than I ken *ye're* good and learned, and no' leein'," said Adam.

"But God might surely reveal to me the truth," replied Mair, "rather than to ten thousand so-called learned men. Babes and sucklings, you know, may receive what is concealed from the great and self-confident."

"My word! ye're neither a babe nor a sucklin',

doctor, as ye ca' yersel'; and, depen' on't, neither am I!" said the Sergeant. "Onyhoo, I think it's mair likely the Almighty wad reveal himsel' to a' the sensible and guid doctors rather than to you alane, forbye a' yer niggers!"

"But I have testimonials of my cures!" continued Dr. Mair.

"Wha kens aboot yer testimonials?" exclaimed Adam. "Could naebody get testimonials but you? And hae ye testimonials frae them ye've kill't? I'se warrant no'! I tell ye again ye'll never pruve tae me that ye're richt and a' the yedicated doctors wrang."

"But it's possible?" asked Dr. Mair, with a smile.

"Possible!" said the Sergeant; "but it's ten thoosand times mair possible that ye're cheatin' yoursel' or cheatin' me. Sae ye may gang."

" But I charge nothing for my attendance, my dear sir, only for the medicine."

"Just so," replied the Sergeant; "sae mony shillings for what maybe didna cost ye a bawbee—pills o' aitmeal or peasebrose. I'm an auld sodger, and canna be made a fule o' that way!"

"I do not depend on my pills so much as on my prayers for the cure of disease," said the quack, solemnly. "Oh, Sergeant! have you no faith in prayer?"

"I houp I hae," replied the Sergeant; "but I hae nae faith in *you*—nane whatsomever!—sae guid day tae ye!"

Dr. Mair packed up his quack medicine in silence, which was meant to be impressive. He sighed, as if in sorrow for human ignorance and unbelief; but seeing no favourable effect produced on the Sergeant he said, "Your blood be on your own unbelieving head! I am free of it."

"Amen!" said the Sergeant; "and gang about yer business to auld wives and idewits, that deserve to dee if they trust the like o' you."

And so the great Dr. Mair departed in wrath—real or pretended—to pursue his calling as a leech, verily, sucking the blood of the credulous, of whom there are not a few among rich and poor, who, loving quackery, are quacked.*

Having disposed of the Quack, we now back into the main line, and resume our journey.

* It may be added as an instructive fact, that such leeches suck at least £300,000 a year out of the people of this country.

# CHAPTER VII.

CORPORAL DICK, who lived in the village of Darnic, several hours' journey by the " Highflyer " coach from Drumsylie, came at this time to pay his annual visit to the Sergeant.

The Corporal, while serving in the same regiment with Adam, had been impressed, as we have already indicated, by the Christian character of his comrade. Those early impressions had been deepened shortly after his return home from service. We need not here record the circumstances in which this decided change in his sentiments and character had taken place. Many of our Scotch readers, at least, have heard of the movement in the beginning of this century by the devoted Haldanes, who, as gentlemen of fortune, and possessing the sincerest and strongest Christian convictions, broke the formality which was freezing Christian life in many a district of Scotland. They did the same kind of work for the Church in the North which Wesley and Whitfield had done for that in the South, though with less permanent results as far as this world is concerned. Dick joined the " Haldanites." Along with all the zeal and strictness characteristic of a small body, he possessed a large share of *bonhomie*, and of the freedom, subdued and regulated, of the old soldier.

At these annual visits the old veterans fought

their battles over again, recalling old comrades and repeating old stories; neither, however, being old in their affections or their memories. But never had the Corporal visited his friend with a more eager desire to "hear his news" than on the present occasion. He had often asked people from Drumsylie, whom he happened to meet, what all this disputing and talk about Adam Mercer meant? And every new reply he received to his question, whether favourable or unfavourable to the Sergeant, only puzzled him the more. One thing, however, he never could be persuaded of—that his friend Adam Mercer would do anything unbecoming to his "superior officer," as he called the minister; or "break the Sabbath," an institution which, like every good Scotchman, he held in peculiar veneration; or be art or part in any mutiny against the ordinances or principles of true religion. And yet, how could he account for all that had been told him by "decent folk" and well-informed persons? The good he heard of the Sergeant was believed in by the Corporal as a matter of course; but what of the evil, which seemed to rest upon equally reliable authority?

Dick must himself hear the details of the "affair," or the battle, as it might turn out.

It was therefore a glad day for both Adam and the Corporal when they again met;—to both a most pleasant change of thought—a glad remembrance of a grand old time already invested with romance—a meeting of men of character, of truth and honour, who could call each other by the loyal name of Friend.

We must allow the reader to fill up the outline which alone we can give of the meeting—the hearty greetings between the two old companions in arms; the minute questions by the one, the full and candid answers by the other; the smiling Katie ever and anon filling up the vacancies left in the narrative of ecclesiastical trials by the Sergeant, from his modesty or want of memory; the joyous satisfaction of Dick, as he found his faith in his comrade vindicated, and saw how firm and impregnable he was in his position, without anything to shake any Christian's confidence in his long-tried integrity, courage, and singleness of heart.

The Corporal's only regret was to see his friend wanting in his usual elasticity of spirits. The fire in his eye was gone, and the quiet yet joyous laugh no longer responded to the old jokes,—a smile being all he could muster. But the Corporal was determined to rouse him. " The wars " would

do it if anything would. And so, when supper
came piping hot, with bubbling half-browned
toasted cheese, mutton pie, tea and toast, followed
by a little whiskey punch, and all without gluttony
or drunkenness, but with sobriety and thankful-
ness felt and expressed—then did the reminiscences begin! And it would be difficult to say
how often the phrase, " D'ye mind, Sergeant?"
was introduced, as old officers and men, old jokes
and old everything—marches, bivouacs, retreats,
charges, sieges, battles—were recalled, with their
anxieties and hardships passed away and their
glory alone remaining.

" Heigho!" the Corporal would say, as he
paused in his excitement, " it's growing a dream
already, Adam! There's no' mony I can speak
tae aboot these auld times;—no' auld to you and
me. Folks' heads are taen up wi' naething but

getting money oot o' the peace we helped to get for the kintra: and little thanks for a' we did—little thanks, little thanks, atweel!" the Corporal would ejaculate in a die-away murmur.

But this was not a time to complain, but to rouse—not to pile arms, but to fire. And so the Corporal said, "Did I tell ye o' the sang made by Sandie Tamson? Ye'll mind Sandie weel—the schulemaster that listed? A maist clever chiel!"

"I mind him fine," said the Sergeant. "Curious eneuch, it was me that listed him! I hae heard a hantle o' his sangs."

"But no' this ane," said Dick, "for he made it—at least he said sae—for our auld Colonel in Perth. It seems Sandie, puir fallow, took to drink—or rather ne'er gied it ower—and sae he cam' beggin' in a kin' o' private genteel way, ye ken, to the Colonel; and when he got siller he wrote

this sang for him.   He gied me a copy for half-
a-crown.   I'll let ye hear 't—altho' my pipe is
no sae guid as yer Sterlin's."

As the Corporal cleared his voice, the Sergeant
lifted the nightcap from his ear, and said, " Sing
awa'."

> Dost thou remember, soldier, old and hoary,
> The days we fought and conquered side by side,
> On fields of battle famous now in story,
> Where Britons triumphed, and where Britons died ?
> Dost thou remember all our old campaigning,
> O'er many a field in Portugal and Spain ?
> Of our old comrades few are now remaining—
> How many sleep upon the bloody plain !
>       Of our old comrades, &c.
>
> Dost thou remember all those marches weary,
> From gathering foes, to reach Corunna's shore ?
> Who can forget that midnight, sad and dreary,
> When in his grave we laid the noble Moore !
> But ere he died our General heard us cheering,
> And saw us charge with vict'ry's flag unfurled ;
> And then he slept, without his ever fearing
> For British soldiers conquering o'er the world.
>       And then he slept,

Rememb'rest thou the bloody Albuera !
The deadly breach in Badajoz's walls !
Vittoria ! Salamanca ! Talavera !
Till Roncesvalles echoed to our balls !
Ha ! how we drove the Frenchmen all before us,
As foam is driven before the stormy breeze !
We fought right on, with conquering banners o'er us,
From Torres Vedras to the Pyrences.
   We fought right on, &c.

Dost thou remember to the war returning,
—Long will our enemies remember too !—
We fought again, our hearts for glory burning,
At Quatre Bras and awful Waterloo !
We thought of home upon that Sabbath morning
When Cameron's pibroch roused our Highland corps,
Then proudly marched, the mighty Emperor scorning,
And vowed to die or conquer as of yore !
   Then proudly marched, &c.

Rememb'rest thou the old familiar faces
Of warriors nursed in many a stormy fight,
Whose lonely graves, which now the stranger traces,
Mark every spot they held from morn till night?
In vain did Cuirassiers in clouds surround them,
With cannon thundering as the tempest raves ;
They left our squares, oh! just as they had found them,
Firm as the rocks amidst the ocean's waves !
   They left our squares, &c.

Those days are past, my soldier, old and hoary,
But still the scars are on thy manly brow ;
We both have shared the danger and the glory,
Come, let us share the peace and comfort now.
Come to my home, for thou hast not another,
And dry those tears, for thou shalt beg no more ;
There, take this hand, and let us march together
Down to the grave, where life's campaign is o'er !
There, take this hand, &c.*

* The words were sung to the French air of—" *Te souviens-tu ?*
*disait un Capitaine :* "—

While the song was being sung the Sergeant turned his head on his pillow away from the Corporal. When it was finished, he said, "Come here, Dick."

The Corporal went to the bed, and seized the Sergeant's proffered hand.

"That sang will do me mair guid than a' their medicine. The guidwife will gie ye half-a-croon for puir Sandie Tamson."

Then asking Katie to leave him alone for a few moments with the Corporal, the Sergeant said, retaining his hand—

"I'm no' dangerously ill, my auld friend; but I'm no weel—I'm no weel! There's a weight on my mind, and an oppression aboot my heart that hauds me doun extraordinar'."

"Dinna gie in, Adam—dinna gie in, wi' the help o' Him that has brocht ye thro' mony a waur fecht," replied the Corporal as he sat down beside him. "D'ye mind the time when ye followed Cainsh up the ladder at Badajoz? and d'ye mind when that glorious fallow Loyd was kill't at Nivelle! Noo——"

"Ah, Dick! thae days, man, are a' by! I'm no' what I was," said the Sergeant. "I'm a puir crippled, wounded veteran, no' fit for ony mair service—no' even as an elder," he added, with a bitter smile.

"Dinna fash yer thoomb, Adam, aboot that business," said Dick. "Ye deserved to hae been drummed oot o' the regiment—I mean the kirk— no' your kirk nor mine, but the kirk o' a' honest and sensible folk, gif ye had swithered aboot that bird. I hae had a crack wi' the cratur, and it's jist extraordinar' sensible like—sae crouse and canty—it wad be like murder tae thraw a neck

like that! In fac', a bird is mair than a bird, I
consider, when it can speak and sing yon way."

"Thank ye, Corporal," said Adam.

"It's some glamour has come ower the minister," said Dick, "just like what cam' ower oor
Colonel, when he made us charge twa thousand
at Busaco, and had, in coorse, tae fa' back on his
supports in disgrace—no' jist in disgrace, for we
never cam' tae that, nor never wull, I hope—but
in confusion!"

"God's wull be done, auld comrade!" replied
Adam; "but it's His wull, I think, that I maun
fa' on the field, and if so, I'm no' feared—na, na!
Like a guid sodger, I wad like tae endure hard-
ness."

"Ye're speakin' ower muckle," interrupted Dick,
"and wearyin' yersel'."

"I maun hae my say oot, Corporal, afore the

forlorn hope marches," continued the Sergeant;
"and as I was remarkin', and because I dinna
want tae be interrupted wi' the affairs o' this
life, so as to please Him wha has ca'd me to
be a sodger—I maun mak' my last wull and
testament noo or never, and I trust you, Dick,
mair than a' the lawyers and law papers i' the
worl', tae see't carried oot." And he held out his
feverish hand to the Corporal, who gave it a re-
sponsive squeeze.

"Ye see, Corporal," said the Sergeant, "I hae
nae fortun' to leave ; but I hae laid by something
for my Katie—and what *she* has been tae me,
God alane kens!" He paused. "And then
there's wee Mary, that I luve amaist as weel as
my Charlie ; and then there's the bird. Na,
Corporal, dinna blame me for speakin' aboot the
bird ! The Apostle, when aboot to be offered up,

spak' aboot his cloak, and nae dead cloak was ever dearer to him than the leevin' bird is tae me, because it was, as ye ken, dear tae the wee fallow that was my ain flesh and bluid, wha's waiting for me. Duve ye mind Charlie?"

"Mind Charlie!" exclaimed the Corporal. "Wait awee, Adam!" and he drew out an old pocket-book from his breast-pocket, from which he took a bit of paper, and unfolding it, held up a lock of silken hair. The Sergeant suddenly seized the relic and kissed it, and then returned it to the Corporal, who, without saying a word, restored it to its old place of safety.

But Dick now began to see that the Sergeant seemed to be rather excited, and no longer able to talk in his usual slow and measured manner; and so he said to him—

"Wait till the morn, Adam, and we'll put a' richt to yer satisfaction."

"Na, na, Corporal!" replied Adam, "I never like pittin' aff—no' a fecht even. What ought to be dune, should be dune when it can—sae listen to me:—Ye'll help Katie tae gaither her siller and gear thegither—it's no' muckle atweel!—and see that she and Mary, wi' the bird, are pit in a bit hoose near yersel'. They can fen' on what I'll lea' them, wi' their ain wark tae help. Ye'll stan' their freen'—I ken, I ken ye wull! And oh, man, when ye hear folk abuse me, dinna say a word in my defence! Let gowans grow frae my grave, and birds sing ower't, and God's sun shine on't, but let nae angry word, against even an enemy, ever be heard frae't, or be conneckit wi' my memory!"

Dick was silent. He felt too much to speak.

The Sergeant continued—"Gie a' my boots and shoon tae Jock Hall. Katie wull tell ye aboot him."

After a pause, he said—"I ask forgiveness o' the minister, if I hae wranged him in ignorance. But as to Smellie—" and the Sergeant turned his head away. "The heart, Corporal," he added, "is hard! I'm no' fit for that yet. God forgie me! but I canna wi'oot hypocrisy say——"

"I'll no' let ye speak another word, Adam!" said Dick. "Trust me as to yer will. I'll be faithfu' unto death!" and he drew himself up, and saluted the Sergeant, soldier fashion.

There was not a bit of the consciously dramatic in this; but he wished to accept the trust given him in due form, as became a soldier receiving important orders from a dying friend.

Adam did not like to confess it ; but he was so wearied that he could speak no more without pain, and so thanking the Corporal, he turned round to sleep.

*i*

# CHAPTER VIII.

## CORPORAL DICK AT THE MANSE.

ADAM had received his pension-paper, which required to be signed by the parish minister, as certifying that the claimant was in life. Dick was glad of this opportunity of calling upon the minister to obtain for his friend the required signature. He was known to Mr. Porteous, who had met him once before in Adam's house, and had attacked him rather sharply on his Haldanite principles, the sect being, as he alleged, an uncalled-for opposition to the regular parish clergy.

,

A short walk brought Dick to the Manse. After a few words of greeting he presented the Sergeant's paper. Mr. Porteous inquired, with rather a sceptical expression on his countenance—

"Is Mr. Mercer really unwell, and unable to come?"

"I have told you the truth, sir," was the Corporal's dignified and short reply.

Mr. Porteous asked what was wrong with him? The Corporal replied that he did not know, but that he was feverish he thought, and was certainly confined to bed.

"Your friend, the Sergeant, as you are probably aware," remarked the minister, signing the paper and returning it to the Corporal, "has greatly surprised and annoyed me. He seems quite a changed man—changed, I fear, for the worse. Oh! yes, Mr. Dick," he continued in reply to a protesting wave of the Corporal's hand, "he is indeed. He has become proud and obstinate—very."

" Meek as a lamb, sir, in time of peace, but brave as a lion in time of war, I can assure you, Mr. Porteous," replied the Corporal.

"I know better!" said the minister.

"Not better than me, sir," replied Dick, "for tho' ye have kent him as well as me, perhaps, in peace, yet ye didna ken him at all in war, and a truer, better, nobler sodger than Adam Mercer never raised his arms to fight or to pray, for he did baith—that I'll say before the worl', and defy contradiction !"

" Remember, Corporal, you and I belong to different Churches, and we judge men differently. We must have discipline. All Churches are not equally pure."

" There's nane o' them pure, wi' your leave,
neither yours nor mine !" exclaimed the Corporal.
" I'm no' pure mysel', and accordingly when I
joined my kirk it was pure nae langer; and, wi'
a' respec' to you, sir, I'm no' sure if your ain
kirk wasna fashed wi' the same diffecculty when
*ye* joined it."

" Discipline, I say, must be maintained—*must*
be," said Mr. Porteous ; " and Adam has come
under it most deservedly. *First* pure, *then*
peaceable, you know."

" If ever a man kept discipline in a regiment,
he did ! My certes !" said Dick, " I wad like
to see him that wad raggle the regiment when
Adam was in't !"

" I am talking of *Church* discipline, sir !" said
the minister, rather irate. " *Church* discipline,
you observe ; which—as I hold yours to be not

a properly constituted Church, but a mere self-constituted sect—you cannot have."

" We're a kin' o' volunteers, I suppose ?" interrupted Dick with a laugh; "the Haldanite volunteers, as ye wad ca' us; but maybe after a' we'll fecht agin the enemy, an' its three corps o' the deevil, the worl', and the flesh, as weel as yours."

" You are not the regular army, anyhow," said the minister, " and I do not recognize your Church."

" The mair's the pity," replied the Corporal, " for I consider it a great blin'ness and misfortin' when ae regiment dislikes anither. An army, minister, is no' ae regiment, but mony. There's cavalry and artillery, light troops and heavy troops, field guns and siege guns in an army, and ilka pairt does its ain wark sae lang as it obeys the commander-in-chief, and fechts for the kingdom. What's the use, then, o' fechtin' agin each ither? In my opinion its real daft like!"

The minister looked impatiently at his watch, but Dick went on to say—

"In Spain, I can tell ye, we were a hantle the better o' thae wild chiels the guerillas. Altho' they didna enlist into the 92nd or ony regular drilled regiment, Scotch or English, the Duke himsel' was thankfu' for them. Noo, Mr. Porteous, altho' ye think us a sort o' guerillas, let us alane,—let us alane!—dinna forbid us tho' we dinna follow *your* flag, but fecht the enemy under oor ain."

"Well, well, Dick, we need not argue about it. My principles are too firm, too long made up, to be shaken at this time of day by the Haldanites," said Mr. Porteous, rising and looking out of the window.

"Weel, weel!" said Dick. "I'm no wantin' to shake your principles, but to keep my ain."

At this stage of the conversation Miss Thomasina entered the room, with "I beg pardon," as if searching for something in the press, but yet for no other purpose, in her eager curiosity, than to ascertain what the Corporal was saying, as she knew him to be a friend of the Sergeant's. Her best attention, with her ear placed close to the door, had made out nothing more than that the rather prolonged conversation had something to do with the great ecclesiastical question of the passing hour in Drumsylie.

Almost breathless with indignation that any one, especially a Haldanite,—for she was quite as "High Church" as her brother,—should presume to take the part of the notorious heretic in the august presence of his great antagonist, she broke in, with what was intended to be a good-humoured smile, but was, to ordinary observers, a bad-natured grin, saying, "Eh! Mr. Dick, *you* to stand up for that man—suspended by the Session, and deservedly so—yes, most deservedly so! Him and his starling, forsooth! It's infidelity at the root."

"It's what?" asked the Corporal, with amazement. "Infidelity did you say, my lady?"

The "my lady" rather softened Miss Thomasina, who returned to the charge more softly, saying, "Well, it's pride and stubbornness, and that's as bad. But I hope his illness will be sanctified to the changing of his heart!" she added, with a sigh, intended to express a very deep concern for his spiritual welfare.

"I hope not, wi' your leave!" replied the Corporal.

"Not wish his heart changed?" exclaimed Miss Thomasina.

"No!" said Dick, emphatically, "not changed, for it's a good Christian heart, and, if changed at all, it wad be changed for the worse."

"A Christian heart, indeed! a heart that would not kill a starling for the sake of the peace of the Session and the Kirk! Wonders will never cease!"

"I hope never," said Dick, "if that's a wonder. Our Lord never killed in judgment man nor beast; and I suppose they were both much about as bad then as now; and His servants should imitate His example, I take it. He was love."

"But," said Mr. Porteous, chiming in, "love is all very well, no doubt, and *ought* to be, where possible; but justice *must* be, love or no love. The one is a principle, the other a feeling."

"I tak' it, with all respect to you, sir, and to madam," said Dick, "that love will aye do what's right, and will, therefore, aye do what's just and generous. We may miss fire pointing the gun wi' the eye o' justice, but never wi' the eye o' love. The sight is then always clearer; anyhow to me. Excuse me, Mr. Porteous, if I presume to preach to you. The Haldanites do a little in that line, tho' they're no' a' ministers! I'm a plain man that speaks my mind, and sin' ye hae gi'en me liberty to speak, let me ax if ye wad hae killed yon fine' bird, that was wee Charlie's, wi' yer ain han', minister?"

"Ay, and all the birds under heaven!" replied Mr. Porteous, "if the law of the Church required it."

"I should think so! and so would I," added Miss Thomasina, walking out of the room.

"It wad be a dreich warl' wi'oot a bird in the wuds or in the lifts!" said the Corporal. "Maybe it's because I'm a Haldanite, but, wi' a' respect, I think I wad miss the birds mair oot o' the warl' than I wad a' the kirk coorts in the kintra!"

"Drop the subject, drop the subject, Mr. Dick!" said the minister, impatiently; "you are getting personal."

The Corporal could not see how that was, but he could see that his presence was not desired. So he rose to depart, saying—"I'm feared I hae been impudent, an' that my gun has got raither het firing, but, in candid truth, I wasna meanin't. But jist let me say ae word mair; ye'll alloo this, that a fool may gie an advice tae a wise man, and this is my advice tae you, sir—

the advice o' an auld sodger and a Haldanite;
no muckle worth, ye may think:—Dinna hairm
Adam Mercer, or ye'll hairm yer best freen', yer
best elder, and yer best parishioner. I beg
pardon for my freedom, sir," he added, with a
deferential bow. The minister returned it stiffly,
remarking only that Mr. Dick was ignorant of
all the facts and history of the case, or he would
have judged otherwise.

Something, however, of what the Corporal had
said fell on the heart of the minister, like dew in
a cloudy night upon dry ground.

# CHAPTER IX.

THE Corporal was obliged, on family or on Haldanite business, we know not which, to return by the "Highflyer" next morning. As that slow but sure conveyance jolted along the road but twice a week, he could not, in the circumstances in which he was placed, remain until its next journey.

On leaving the Manse, he proceeded at once to the house of Dr. Scott, the well-known doctor of the parish, and of a district around it limited only by the physical endurance of himself and of his brown horse, "Bolus." When the

Corporal called, the Doctor was absent on one of his constantly recurring professional rides. Being a bachelor, his only representative was his old servant Effie, who received the visitor. She kept the surgery as well as the house, and was as well known in the parish as her master. Indeed she was suspected by many to have skill equal to her master's, very likely owing to the powerful effects produced by her suggestive prescriptions. On learning the absence of the doctor, the Corporal inquired when he was likely to return.

"Wha i' the worl' can tell that? Whatna quastion tae speer at me!" exclaimed Effie.

"I meant nae offence," replied the Corporal; "but my freend, Sergeant Mercer——"

"I beg yer pardon," interrupted Effie; "I wasna awar that ye were a freen' o' the Sergeant's, honest man! Sae I may tell *you* that the

doctor may be here in a minute, or maybe no'
till breakfast-time the morn; or he may come
at twal', at twa, or Gude kens whan! But if
it's an *ordinar'* thing ye want for yersel' or
Adam, I can gie 't to ye :—sic as a scoorin' dose
o' sauts or castur-ile, or rubhard pills, or seena
leaf, or even a flee blister; or a few draps o'
lodamy for the grips."

The Corporal listened with all respect, and
said, "I want naething for mysel' or Adam; but
Dr. Scott is requested to veesit him on his
return hame, or as soon after as convenient."

"Convenient!" exclaimed Effie, "that's no' a
word kent in Drumsylie for the doctor! He
micht as well ax every gudewife in the parish
if it was convenient for them to hae a son or
a dochter at twal' hours i' the day or at twal'
at nicht, on a simmer's day or on a snawy ane;

or tae ax whan it was convenient for folk tae
burn their fit, break their leg, or play the
mishanter wi' themsels efter a fair. Convenient!
Keep us a'! But depen' on't he'll mak' it
convenient tae atten' Mr. Mercer, nicht or mornin',
sune or early."

"I'm sorry to trouble him, for I am sure
he is unco' bothered and fashed," said the
Corporal, politely.

"Fashed!" exclaimed Effie, thankful for the
opportunity of expressing sympathy with her
master, and her indignation at his inconsiderate
patients; "Naebody kens that but him and me!
Fashed! the man haesna the life o' a streyed
dog or cat! There's no' a lameter teylor wi' his
waik fit, nor a bairn wi' a sair wame frae eatin'
ower mony cruds or grosats, nor an auld wife
hostin' wi' a grew o' cauld, nor a farmer efter

makin' ower free wi' black puddins and haggis when a mairt is kill't—but a' maun flce tae the doctor, ilka ane yam, yam, yammerin', as if *he* had the poower o' life and death! Puir cratur! I could maist greet if I wasna sae angry, to wauk him in his first sleep in a winter's nicht to ride aff on auld Bolus—that's his auld decent horse, ye ken—and for what? Maybe for naething! I assure you he has a taughy fleece tae scoor in this parish!" Effie stopped, not from want of illustration, but from want of breath.

"A hard life, a hard life, nae doot," remarked the Corporal ; "but it's his duty, and he's paid for't."

"Him paid for't!" said Effie, "I wad like tae see the siller; as the watchmaker said—The Doctor, quo' he, should let them pay the debt o' natur' if they wadna pay his ain debts first. He wasna far wrang! But I was forgettin' the Sergeant—

what's wrang wi' him? That's a man never
fashes the doctor or onybody; and wha pays
what he gets. But ither folk fash the Sergeant
—I wuss I had the doctorin' o' some o' them
I ken o'! Feggs, I wad doctor them! I wad gie
them a blister or twa o' Spenish flees that they
wadna forget in a hurry!—but what's wrang?"
she asked, once more halting in her eloquence.

"That's just what we want tae ken," replied
the Corporal, quietly.

"I'll tell the Doctor," said Effie. "I think
ye said yer name was Dick—Cornal Dick?"

"No, no! not Cornal yet," replied Dick,
smiling, "I'm sorry tae say, my braw woman,
but Corporal only."

The epithet "braw" drew down a curtsy from
Effie in reply to his "Gude day; ye'll be sure
to send the Doctor."

Dr. Scott, whom Effie represented, was a man of few words, who never attempted to explain the philosophy, if he knew it, of his treatment, but prescribed his doses as firmly and unfeelingly as the gunner loads his cannon. He left his patients to choose life or death, apparently as if their choice was a matter of indifference to him : yet nevertheless he possessed a most kind and feeling heart, revealed not in looks or words, but in deeds of patience and self-sacrifice, for which, from too many, he got little thanks, and less pay, as Effie had more than insinuated. Every one in the parish seemed to have a firm conviction as to the duty of the doctor to visit them, when unwell, at all hours, and at all distances, by day or night; while *their* duty of consideration for his health was dim, and for his pocket singularly procrastinating. " I do not grudge," he once said, "to give my professional aid gratis to the poor and needy, and even to others who could pay me if they would ; nay, I do not grudge in many cases to send a bag of meal to the family, but I think I am entitled without being considered greedy, and without my sending for it, to get my empty bag returned ! "

The doctor was ever riding to and fro, his face red with winter's cold and summer's heat, nodding oftener on his saddle than at his own fire-side, watching all sorts of cases in farm-houses and lowly cottages, cantering for miles to the anxiety and discomforts of . the sick-room.

All liked the Doctor, and trusted him ; though, alas ! such men as Dr. Mair—herbalists, vendors of wonderful pills and "saws," bone-setters, and that whole race of ignorant and presuming quacks, resident or itinerant, could always impose on the credulous, and dispose of their marvellous cures for such prices as seldom entered honest Scott's pocket.

The doctor in due time visited Adam.

"What's wrong, Sergeant?" was his abrupt question ; and he immediately proceeded to examine tongue and pulse, and other signs and symptoms. He then prescribed some simple medicine, rather gentler than Effie's ; and said little, except that he would call back soon. The case was at last declared to be of a bad type of typhoid fever.

# CHAPTER X.

MR. SMELLIE was not only a draper, but was the greatest in that line in the parish of Drumsylie. His shop had the largest display of goods in the village. Handkerchiefs, cravats, Paisley shawls, printed calicoes, &c. streamed in every variety of colour from strings stretched across the large window, dotted with hats and bonnets for male and female customers. He was looked upon as a well-to-do, religious man, who carefully made the most of both worlds. He was a bachelor, and lived in a very small house, above his shop, which was reached by a screw stair. A small charity boy, with a singularly sedate countenance—he may for aught I know be now a rich merchant on the London Exchange—kept the shop. I mention his name, Eben or Ebenezer Peat, to preserve for some possible biographer the important part which the as yet great unknown played in his early life. The only domestic was old Peggy ; of whom, beyond her name, I know nothing. She may have been great, and no doubt was, if she did her duty with zeal and love to Peter Smellie. Peggy inhabited the kitchen, and her master the parlour, attached to which was a small bed closet. The parlour was cold and stiff, like a cell for a condemned Pharisee. There was little furniture in it save an old sofa, whose hard bony skeleton was covered by a cracked skin of black haircloth, with a small round cushion of the same character, roughened by rather bristly hairs, which lay in a recess at the end of it. A few stuffed mahogany chairs were ranged along the wall; while a very uncomfortable arm-chair beside the small fire, and a round table with a dark wax-cloth cover, completed the furniture of the apartment. There were, besides, a few old books of theology—which guaranteed Mr. Smellie's orthodoxy, if not his reading; a copy of "Buchan's Domestic Medicine," and a sampler which hung on the wall, sewed by his only sister, long dead, on which was worked a rude symbol of Castle Bennock with three swans floating under it, nearly as large as the castle, and beneath what was intended to represent flowers, were the symbols "For P. S. by M. S."

Mr. Smellie, near a small fire, that twinkled like a yellow cairngorm amidst basalt, sat reading his newspaper, when a letter was laid upon his table by Peggy without any remark except, "A letter."

"From whom, Peggy?" asked Smellie.

"Dinna ken; was left on the coonter."

Mr. Smellie opened it. No sooner did he recognise the signature, than he laid aside the paper—the *Edinburgh Courant*, even then best known and long established.

He read the letter over and over again, very possibly a hundred times if one might judge from the time it remained in his hands. At last he put it down quietly, as if afraid it would make a noise, and stared at the small embryo fire. He then paced across the room; lay down on the sofa; resumed his seat at the fire; took up the letter, again perused it, and again slowly laid it down. He alone could decipher his own thoughts while doing all this. For a time he was confused and bewildered, as if endeavouring to comprehend his altered position. It was to him as if some one whom he had hanged or murdered had come to life again. What was he to do now with reference to the Sergeant? This was what puzzled him—what could be done to save himself? He had felt safe in the hands of an honourable man—at a distance. He had in fact, during many years of comparative ease as to worldly things, almost forgotten his old attempt at cheating. He had long ago repented, as he thought, of his crime ; but that which was past had now risen from the dead, and God seemed to require it at his hands !

Had not his own continued sinfulness thus restored the dead past to life?

It was a great shock for him to learn for

the first time that his enemy, as he looked upon Adam, knew it all, and had him in his power. And then to learn also that the Sergeant had never divulged the secret! What could Smellie now do? Would he provoke Adam to blast his character, to triumph over him, to expose him to the Kirk Session and the parish? nay, to—to banish him! Or would he repent truly of all that false, hollow past which was now being dimly revealed to him; confess his evil-doing to the Sergeant, and ask his forgiveness, as well as that of God; trust his mercy, bless him for his generosity, acknowledge that he was the better man, and seek by a new and true life to imitate him? O Mr. Smellie! this is indeed one of those moments in thy life in which a single step to the right or left may lead thee to light or to darkness, to heaven or to

hell. Thy soul, of immeasurable littleness estimated by the world, but of infinite greatness
estimated by eternal truth and righteousness, is
now engaged in a battle in which its eternal
destiny is likely to be determined! Confront
then the good and evil masters, God and Mam-
mon, who are contending for the mastery; serve
the one and despise the other, and even thou
mayest yet be great because good. But if not!
—then in a few minutes mayest thou be irreco-
verably on the road to thine own place; and
though this will be nothing to Drumsylie, it will
be everything to thee!

The battle went hard against Saul, and the
Philistines of vanity, pride, and a wicked consistency were pressing hard upon him! One
thing only, the easiest for the time, he determined to do, and that was to get out of the

scrape—as his bad angel soothingly suggested
—as speedily and as easily as possible. He
must not keep up the quarrel longer with the
Sergeant; this at least seemed clear: for such
a course was dangerous. He must also immediately assure John Spence of obedience to his
commands. So, without delay, he wrote to the
keeper, imploring him, as he himself expected
mercy from God, to be silent regarding the old
crime; assuring him that he had mistaken the
part which he had taken as an elder in this most
painful case, as he called it, and promising him
to do all he could to deliver the Sergeant out
of trouble, which would be at once his duty and
his pleasure. This letter, when written and
despatched, was a great relief to his mind: it
delivered him, as he hoped, from immediate
danger at least, and enabled him to concentrate

his acute faculties on the carrying out of his plans for securing his own safety.

His thoughts were for the moment broken by Eben announcing, as he was wont to do, a superior customer whom it was expedient for the master himself to serve. The customer on the present occasion was Miss Thomasina Porteous, who had come to purchase some article for herself, and a cheap shawl, out of the Session Charity Fund, for their poor, persecuted, common friend, as she called Mrs. Craigie.

Mr. Smellie was unusually silent: he did not respond to the order for Mrs. Craigie with his accustomed smile. After a little, Miss Thomasina blandly remarked :—" Sergeant Mercer is very ill, and I have no doubt from a bad conscience —there's no peace, you know, Mr. Smellie, to the wicked."

"I am aware!" said Mr. Smellie, drily. "This cheap shawl," he added, selecting and spreading out one before her, "is good enough, I suppose, for a pauper?"

"Considering all she has suffered from that man, I think she should get a better one, or something in addition, Mr. Smellie," said the lady.

"Eben!" said Smellie, "go up-stairs. I wish to speak to Miss Porteous alone."

The boy disappeared.

"As a friend, Miss Porteous," whispered Smellie, "permit me to say, *in strictest confidence* —you understand?—"

"Quite!" replied Miss Thomasina, with a look of intense curiosity.

"That I have learned some things about Mrs Craigie," continued Mr. Smellie, "which should make us *extremely* cautious in helping or trusting her."

"Indeed!" said Miss Thomasina.

"And as regards the Sergeant," said Mr. Smellie, "there is—rightly or wrongly is not the question—a strong sympathy felt for him in the parish.   It is human nature to feel, you know, for the weak side, even if it is the worst side; and from my profound respect for our excellent minister, over whom you exercise such great and useful influence, I would advise——"

"That he should yield, Mr. Smellie?" interrupted Miss Thomasina, with an expression of wonder.

"No, no, Miss Porteous," replied the worthy Peter, "that may be impossible; but that we should allow Providence to deal with Adam.   He is ill.   The Doctor, I heard to-day, thinks it may come to typhus fever. He is threatened, at least."

"And may die?" said the lady, interpreting the elder's thoughts. "But I hope not, poor man, for his own sake. It would be a solemn judgment!"

"I did not say die," continued Smellie; "but many things may occur—such as repentance— a new mind, &c. Anyhow," he added with a smile, "he should, in my very humble opinion, be dealt wi' charitably—nay, I would say kindly. Our justice should be tempered wi' mercy, so that no enemy could rejoice over us, and that we should feel a good conscience—the best o' blessings," he said with a sigh—"as knowing that we had exhausted every means o' bringing him to a right mind; for, between us baith, and knowing your Christian principles, I do really

houp that at heart he is a good man. Forgie
me for hinting it, as I would not willingly pain
you, but I really believe it. Now, if he dees,
we'll have no blame. So I say, or rather
suggest, that, wi' your leave, we should in the
meantime let things alone, and say no more
about this sad business. I leave you to propose
this to our worthy minister."

"I think *our* kindness and charity, Mr. Smellie,"
replied Miss Porteous, "are not required at present. On my word, no! My poor brother requires
both, not Mercer. See how *he* is petted! Those
upstart Gordons have been sending him, I hear,
all sorts of good things: wine and grapes—grapes,
that even I have only tasted once in my life, when
my mother died! And Mrs. Gordon called on him
yesterday in her carriage! It's absolutely ridi-
culous! I would even say an insult! tho' I'm

sure I don't wish the man any ill—not I ; but only that we must not spoil him, and make a fool of my brother and the Session, as if Mercer was innocent. I assure you my brother feels this sort of mawkish sympathy very much—very much. It's mean and cowardly!"

"It is quite natural that he should feel annoyed," replied Mr. Smellie; "and so do I. But nevertheless, I again say we must be merciful; for mercy rejoiceth over judgment. So I humbly advise to let things alone for the present, and to withdraw our hand when Providence begins to work;—in the meantime, in the meantime."

Miss Thomasina was not prepared for these new views on the part of the high-principled, firm, and consistent elder. They crossed her purpose. She had no idea of giving up the battle in this easy way. What had she to do with Providence ? To stand firm and fast to her principles was, she had ever been taught, the one thing needful; and until the Sergeant confessed his fault, it seemed to her, as she said, that "he should be treated as a heathen and a publican!"

Mr. Smellie very properly put in the saving clause, "But no waur—no waur, Miss Porteous." He also oiled his argument by presenting his customer with a new pair of gloves out of a parcel just received from Edinburgh, as evidence of his admiration for her high character.

The lady smiled and left the shop, and said she would communicate the substance of their conversation to her brother.

"Kindly, kindly, as becomes your warm heart," said Mr. Smellie, expressing the hope at the same time that the gloves would fit her fingers as well as he wished his arguments would fit the mind of Mr. Porteous.

Another diplomatic stroke of Mr. Smellie in his extremity was to obtain the aid of his easy brother-elder, Mr. Menzies, to adjust matters with the Sergeant, so as to enable Mr. Porteous, with some show of consistency, to back out of the ecclesiastical mess in which the Session had become involved: for "consistency" was a great idol in the Porteous Pantheon.

"I hae been thinking, my good freen'," said Smellie to Menzies, as both were seated beside the twinkling gem of a fire in the sanctum over the draper's shop, "that possibly—possibly—we micht men' matters atween the Session and Sergeant Mercer. He is verra ill, an' the thocht is neither pleasant nor satisfactory to us that he should dee—a providential event which *micht* happen—an' wi' this scandal ower his head. I am willin', for ane, to do whatever is reasonable in the case, and I'm sure sae are ye; for ye ken, Mr. Menzies, there's nae man perfec'—nane! The fac' is, I'm no' perfec' mysel'!" confessed Mr. Smellie, with a look intended to express a humility of which he was profoundly unconscious.

Mr. Menzies, though not at all prepared for this sudden outburst of charity, welcomed it very sincerely. "I'm glad," said he, "to hear a man o' your influence in the Session say sae." Menzies had himself personally experienced to a large degree the *dour* influence of the draper over him; and, though his better nature had often wished to rebel against it, yet the logical meshes of his more astute and strong-willed brother had hitherto entangled him. But now, with the liberty of speech granted in so genial a manner by Smellie, Mr. Menzies said, "I wull admit that Mr. Mercer was, until this unfortunate business happened, a maist respectable man—I mean he was apparently, and I wad fain houp sincerely—a quiet neebour, and a douce elder. I never had cause to doot him till the day ye telt me in confidence that he had been ance a poacher. But we mauna be ower hard, Mr. Smellie, on the sins o' youth, or even o' riper years. Ye mind the paraphrase—

> " ' For while the lamp holds on to burn,
>     The greatest sinner may return.'

I wad do onything that was consistent to get him oot o' this job wi' the minister an' the Session. But hoo can it be managed, Mr. Smellie ? "

"I think," said Smellie, meditatively, "that if we could only get the minister pleased, things wad richt themsel's."

"Between oorsel's, as his freen's," said Menzies, with a laugh, "he's no' easy to please when he tak's a thraw! But maybe we're as muckle to blame as him."

"That bird," remarked Smellie, as he poked up his almost extinguished fire, "has played a' the mischief! Could we no' get it decently oot o' the way yet, Mr. Menzies?"

"What d'ye mean, neebour?" asked Menzies, looking puzzled.

"Weel, I'll tell ye," replied the draper. "The Sergeant and me, ye ken, cast oot; but you and him, as well as the wife, are freendly. Noo, what do ye say to seeing them in a freendly way; and as the Sergeant is in bed——"

"They say it's fivver," interrupted Menzies, "and may come to be verra dangerous."

"Weel a-weel," said Smellie, "in that case what I propose micht be easier dune: the wife micht gie you the bird, for peace' sake—for conscience' sake—for her guidman's sake—and ye micht do awa' wi't, and the Sergeant ken naething about it; for, ye see, being an auld sodger, he's prood as prood can be; and Mr. Porteous wad be satisfied, and maybe, for peace' sake, wad never speer hoo it was dune, and we wad' hae a guid excuse for sayin' nae mair about it in the Session. If the Sergeant dee'd, nae hairm would be done; if he got weel, he wad be thankfu' that the stramash was a' ower, and himsel' restored, wi'oot being pit aboot for his bird. Eh?"

"I wadna like to meddle wi' the cratur," said Menzies, shaking his head.

"But, man, do ye no' see," argued Smellie, "that it wad stultify yersel' tae refuse doing what is easier for you than for him? Hoo can ye, as a member o' Session, blame him for no' killing a pet o' his dead bairn, if ye wadna kill it as a strange bird?"

"Can *ye* no' kill't then?" asked Menzies.

"I wad hae nae difficulty in doing that— nane," said Smellie, "but they wadna trust me, and wadna lippen to me; but they wad trust *you*. It's surely your duty, Mr. Menzies, to do this, and mair, for peace."

"Maybe," said Menzies. "Yet it's a cruel job. I'm sweir tae meddle wi't. I'll think aboot it."

"Ay," said Smellie, putting his hand on his shoulder; "an' ye'll do't, too, when ye get the opportunity—I dinna bid ye kill't, that needna be ; but jist tae let it flee awa'—that's the plan ! Try't. I'm awfu' keen to get this job by, an' this stane o' offence oot o' the road. But mind, ye'll never, never, let on I bade ye, or it will blaw up the mercifu' plan. Will ye keep a quiet sough aboot me, whatever ye do ? And, moreover, never breathe a word about the auld poaching business ; I hae reasons for this, Mr. Menzies—reasons."

Such was Smellie's "game," as it may be called. For his own ends he was really anxious that Mr. Porteous should feel kindly towards the Sergeant, so far at least as to retrace the steps he had taken in his case. He was actuated by fear lest Adam, if crushed, should be induced to turn against himself, and, in revenge, expose his former dishonest conduct.

He did not possess necessarily any gratitude for the generous part which Adam had played towards him ;—for nothing is more hateful to a proud man, than to be under an obligation to one whom he has injured. It was also very doubtful how far Mr. Porteous, from the strong and public position he had taken in the case, would, or could yield, unless there was opened up to him some such back-door of escape as Smellie was contriving, to save his consistency. If this could be accomplished without himself being implicated, Smellie saw some hope of ultimate reconciliation, and the consequent removal on the Sergeant's part of the temptation to " peach."

Mr. Menzies, however, was ill at ease. The work Smellie had assigned to him was not agreeable, and he was only induced to attempt its performance in the hope that the escape of the starling would lead ultimately to the quashing of all proceedings against Adam.

With these feelings he went off to call upon Mrs. Mercer.

# CHAPTER XI.

MRS. MERCER received her visitor very coldly. She associated his name with what she called " the conspiracy," and felt aggrieved that he had never visited her husband during those previous weeks of trial. He was, as she expressed it, "a sight for sair een." Mr. Menzies made the best excuse he could, and described the circumstances in which he had been placed towards Adam as the reason why he had not visited her sooner. He said, also, that however painful it was to him, he had nevertheless been obliged by his ordination vows to do his duty as a member of Session, and he hoped not in vain, as he might now be the means of making peace between his friend, Mr. Mercer, and the minister.

"I'm Charlie's bairn," said the starling, just as Menzies had given a preliminary cough, and was about to approach the question which had chiefly brought him to the cottage. "I'm Charlie's bairn—a man's a man—kick kur—whitt, whitt."

The starling seemed unable or unwilling to end the sentence; at last it came out clear and distinct—"a man's a man for a' that."

Mr. Menzies did not feel comfortable.

"I dinna wunner, Mrs. Mercer," at last he said, "at you and Adam likin' that bird! He *is* really enticing, and by ordinar, I maun confess."

"There's naething wrang wi' the bird," said Katie, examining the seam of her apron, adding in an indifferent tone of voice, "If folk wad only let it alane, it's discreet, and wad hairm naebody."

"I'm sure, Mrs. Mercer," he said, "I'm real sorry about the hale business; and I'm resolved, if possible, to get Adam oot o' the han's o' the Session, and bring peace atween a' parties."

Katie shook her foot, twirled her thumbs, but said nothing.

"It's a pity indeed," the elder continued, "that a *bird* should come atween an office-bearer like Adam, and his minister and the Session! It's no richt—it's no richt; and yet neither you nor Adam could pit it awa, e'en at the request o' the Session, wi' yer ain haun's. Na, na—that *was* askin' ower muckle."

"Ye ken best, nae doot," said Katie, with a touch of sarcasm in her voice. "You and the Session hae made a bonnie job o' the guidman noo!"

"I'm real vexed he's no' weel," said Menzies; "but to be candid, Mrs. Mercer, it wasna a' the faut o' the Session at the warst, but pairtly his ain. He was ower stiff, and was neither to haud nor bin'."

"A bairn could haud him noo, and bin' him tae," said Katie.

"There's a chasteesement in 't," remarked Menzies, becoming slightly annoyed at Katie's cool reception of him. "He should hear the voice in the rod. Afflictions dinna come wi'oot a reason. They spring not from the grun'. They're sent for a purpose; and ye should examine and search yer heart, Mrs. Mercer, in

a' sincerity and humility, to ken *why* this affliction has come, and *at this time*," emphatically
added Mr. Menzies.

"Nae doot," said Katie, returning to the hem
of her apron.

The way seemed marvellously opened to Mr.
Menzies, as he thought he saw Katie humbled
and alive to the Sergeant's greater share of
wrong in causing the schism. He began to feel
the starling in his hand,—a fact of which the
bird seemed ignorant, as he whistled, "Wha'll
be king but Charlie!"

Mr. Menzies continued—"If I could be ony help
to ye, Mrs. Mercer, I wad be prood and thankfu'
to bring aboot freen'ship atween Adam and Mr.
Porteous ; and thus gie peace to puir Adam."

"Peace tae Adam?" exclaimed Katie, looking
up to the elder's face.

"Ay, peace tae Adam," said Mr. Menzies, encouraged to open up his plan; "but, I fear, as lang as that bird is in the cage, peace wull never be."

Katie dropped her apron, and stared at Mr. Menzies as if she was petrified, and asked what he meant.

"Dinna think, dinna think," said Mr. Menzies, "that I propose killin' the bit thing"—Katie dropped her eyes again on her apron—"but," he continued, "I canna see what hairm it wad do, and I think it wad do a hantle o' guid, if ye wad let me tak' oot the cage, and let the bird flee awa' tae sing wi' the lave o' birds. In this way, ye see—— "

Katie rose up, her face pale with—dare we say it?—suppressed passion. This call of Menzies was to give strength and comfort, forsooth, to her in her affliction! She seized the elder by his arm, drew him gently to the door of the bed-room, which was so far open as to enable him to see Adam asleep. One arm of the Sergeant was extended over the bed, his face was towards them, his grey locks escaped from under his night-cap, and his expression was calm and composed. Katie said nothing, but pointed to her husband and looked sternly at Menzies. She then led him to the street door, and whispered in his ear—

"Ae word afore we pairt:—I wadna gie that man, in health or sickness, life or death, for a' the Session! If *he's* no' a Christian, an' if *he* hasna God's blessing, wae's me for the warl'! I daur ony o' ye to come here again, and speak ill o' him, as if he was in a faut! I daur ony o' ye to touch his bird! Tell that to Smellie— tell't to the parish, and lee me alane wi' my

ain heart, wi' my ain guidman, and wi' my ain
Saviour, to live or dee as the Almighty wills!"

Katie turned back into her kitchen, while poor
Menzies walked out into the street, feeling no
anger but much pain, and more than ever con-
vinced that he had been made a tool of by
Smellie, contrary to his own common-sense and
better feeling.

Menzies made a very short report of the scene
to the draper, saying that he would wash his
hands clean of the whole business; to which
Smellie only said to himself thoughtfully, as
Menzies left his shop, "I wish I could do the
same—but I'll try!"

# CHAPTER XII.

D<sup>R.</sup> SCOTT, as the reader knows, had visited Adam, and felt a great interest in his patient. The Doctor was a man of few words, very shy, and, as has been indicated, even abrupt and gruff, his only affectation being his desire to appear devoid of any feeling which might seem to interfere with severe medical treatment or a surgical operation. He liked to be thought stern and decided. The fact was that his intense sympathy pained him, and he tried to steel himself against it. When he scolded his patients it was because they made him suffer so much, and because, moreover, he was angry with himself for being angry with them. He therefore affected unconcern at the very time when his anxiety for a patient made him sleepless, and compelled him often, when in bed, to read medical journals with the aid of a long yellow candle, instead of spending in sleep such portions of his night-life as the sick permitted him to enjoy. He had watched Adam's whole conduct as an elder— had heard much about his labours from his village patients—and, as the result of his observations, had come to the conclusion that he was a man of a rare and right stamp. When the " disturbance," as it was called, about the Starling agitated the community, few ever heard the Doctor express his opinion on the great question ; but many listened to his loud laugh—wondering as to its meaning—when the case was mentioned and how oddly he stroked his chin, as if to calm his merriment. Some friends who were more in his confidence heard him utter such phrases, in alluding to the matter, as—"only ministerial indigestion," "ecclesiastical hysteria,"—forms of evil, by the way, which are rarely dealt with in Church courts.

His attendance on the Sergeant was, therefore, a duty which was personally agreeable to him. He was not very hopeful of success, however, from the time when the fever developed into typhoid of a malignant and extremely infectious type.

The first thing which the Doctor advised as being necessary for the Sergeant's recovery, was the procuring of a sick-nurse. Poor Katie protested against the proposal. What could any one do, she argued, that she herself was not fit for? What cared she for sleep? She never

indeed at any time slept soundly—so she alleged
—and could do with very little sleep at all times;
she was easily wakened up—the scratch of a
mouse would do it; and Adam would do *her*
bidding, for he was always so good and kind: a
stranger, moreover, would but irritate him, and
"put hersel' aboot." And who could be got to
assist? Who would risk their life? Had not
others their own family to attend to? Would
they bring the fever into their own house? &c.
"Na, na," she concluded, "lee Adam tae me, and
God will provide!"

So she reasoned, as one taught by observation and experience; for most people in country
villages—now as then—are apt to be seized with
panic in the presence of any disease pronounced
to be dangerous and contagious. Its mystery
affects their imagination. It looks like a doom

that cannot be averted ;—a very purpose of God, to oppose which is vain. To procure, therefore, a nurse for the sick, except among near relations, is extremely difficult; unless it be some worthless creature who will drink the wine intended for the patient, or consume the delicacies left for his nourishment. We have known, when cholera broke out in a county town in Scotland, a stranger nurse refused even lodgings in any house within it, lest she should spread the disease !

It was a chill and gusty evening, and Katie sat beside the fire in the Sergeant's room, her mind full of "hows" and "whens," and tossed to and fro by anxiety about her Adam, and questionings as to what she should or could do for his comfort. The rising wind shook the bushes and tree-tops in the little garden. The dust in clouds hurried along the street of the village. The sky was dark with gathering signs of rain. There was a depressing sadness in the world without, and little cheer in the room within. The Sergeant lay in a sort of uneasy restless doze, sometimes tossing his hands, starting up and asking where he was, and then falling back again on his pillow with a heavy sigh. Although his wife was not seriously alarmed, she was nevertheless very miserable at heart, and felt unutterably lonely. But for her quiet faith in God, and the demand made upon her for active exertion, she would have yielded to passionate grief, or fallen into sullen despair.

Her thoughts were suddenly disturbed by little Mary telling her that some one was at the street door. Bidding Mary take her place, she hastened to the kitchen and opened the door. Jock Hall entered, in his usual unceremonious way.

"Ye needna speak, Mistress Mercer," he said as he sat down on a chair near the door; "I ken a' aboot it!"

Katie was as much startled as she was the first time he entered her house. His appearance as to dress and respectability was, however, unquestionably improved.

"Jock Hall, as I declare!" exclaimed Katie in a whisper.

"The same, at yer service; and yet no' jist the same," replied Jock, in as low a voice.

"Ye may say sae," said Katie. "What's come ower ye? Whaur hae ye been? Whaur got ye thae claes? Ye're like a gentleman, Jock!"

"I houp sae," replied Hall; "I oucht to be sae; I gat a' this frae Adam."

"The guidman?" inquired Katie; "that's impossible! He never had claes like thae!"

" Claes or no claes," said Jock, " it's him I got them frae."

" I dinna understan' hoo that could be," said Katie.

" Nor me," said Jock ; " but *sae* it is, and never speer the noo *hoo* it is. I'm come, as usual, on business."

" Say awa'," said Katie, " but speak laigh. It's no' shoon ye're needin', I houp ? "

But we must here explain that Jock had previously called upon Dr. Scott, and thrusting his head into the surgery—his body and its new dress being concealed by the half-opened door—asked—

" Is't true that Sergeant Mercer has got a smittal fivver ? "

The Doctor, who was writing some prescription, on discovering who the person was who put this

question, said no more in reply than—" Deadly !
deadly ! so ye need not trouble them, Jock, by
begging at their door—be off ! "

" Mrs. Mercer," replied Jock, "wull need a nurse
—wull she ? "

"You had better go and get your friend Mrs.
Craigie for her, if that's what you are after.   She'll
help Mary," replied the doctor, in derision.

" Thank ye ! " said Jock, and disappeared.

But to return to his interview with Mrs. Mercer.
—" I'm telt, Mrs. Mercer," he said, " that the Sergeant is awfu' ill wi' a smittal fivver, and that he
needs some nurse—that is, as I understan', some
ane that wad watch him day and nicht, and keep
their een open like a whitrat ; somebody that
wadna heed haein' muckle tae do, and that could
haud a guid but freen'ly grip o' Mr. Mercer gif
his nerves rise.   An' I hae been thinkin' ye'll fin't

a bother tae get sic a bodie in Drumsylie—unless, maybe, ane that wad wark for a hantle o' siller; some decent woman like Luckie Craigie, wha micht——"

" Dinna bother me the noo, Jock, wi' ony nonsense," said Katie, " I'm no fit for't. If ye need onything yersel', tell me what it is, and, if possible, I'll gie ye't. But I maun gang back tae the room."

" Ay," said Jock, "I want something frae ye, nae doot, and I houp I'll get it. I want an extraordinar' favour o' ye ; for, as I was sayin', ye'll fin't ill tae get ony ane to watch Mr. Mercer. But if *I* get ane that doesna care for their life — that respecs and loes Adam—that wadna take a bawbee o' siller——"

" As for that o't, I'll pay them decently," interrupted Katie.

" And ane that," continued Jock, as if not inter-

rupted, " has strength tae watch wi' leevin' man or
woman,—what wad ye say tae sic a canny nurse
as that ? "

" If there's sic a bodie in the toon," replied
Katie, " I wad be blythe tae *try* them ; no' tae fix
them, maybe, but to *try*, as the Doctor insists
on't."

" Weel," said Jock, " the favour I hae to ax,
altho' its ower muckle maybe for you tae gie,
is to let *me* try my han' — let me speak, and
dinna lauch at me ! I'm no feered for death, as
I hae been mony a time feered for life ; I hae
had by ordinar' experience watchin', ye ken, as a
poacher, fisher, and a' that kin' o' thing, sin' I
was a bairn ; sae I can sleep wi' my een open ;
and I'm strong, for I hae thrashed keepers,
and teylors, and a' sorts o' folk ; fac', I was
tempted tae gie a blue ee tae Smellie !—but let

sleepin' dogs lie—I'll mak' a braw nurse for the gude man."

Katie was taken so much aback by this speech as to let Jock go on without interruption ; but she at last exclaimed—" Ye're a kind cratur, Jock, and I'm muckle obleeged to you ; but I really canna think o't. It 'ill no' work ; it wad pit ye aboot, an' mak' a cleish-me-claver in the toon ; an'—an'——"

" I care as little for the toon," said Jock, " as the toon cares for me ! Ye'll no' be bothered wi' me, mind, gif ye let me help ye. I hae got clean pease strae for a bed frae Geordie Miller the carrier, and a sackfu' for a bowster ; and I ken ye hae a sort o' laft, and I'll pit up there ; and it's no aften I hae sic a bed ; and cauld parritch or cauld praties wull dae for my meat, an' I need nae mair ; an' I hae braw thick stockin's—I can pit on twa pair if necessar', tae walk as quiet as a cat stealin' cream ;

sae gif ye'll let me, I'll do my best endeevour tae help ye."

" Oh, Jock, man !" said Mrs. Mercer, "ye're unco' guid. I'll think o't—I'll think o't, and speer at the Doctor—I wull, indeed ; and if sae be he needs—Whisht ! What's that ?" ejaculated Katie, starting from her chair, as little Mary entered the kitchen hurriedly, saying—

" Come ben fast, mither !"

Katie was in a moment beside her husband, who for the first time manifested symptoms of violent excitement, declaring that he must rise and dress for church, as he heard the eight o'clock bells ringing. In vain she expostulated with him in the tenderest manner. He ought to rise, he said, and would rise. Was he not an elder ? and had he not to stand at the plate ? and would he, for any consideration, be late ? What did she mean? Had she lost her senses? And so on.

This was the climax of a weary and terribly anxious time for Katie. For some nights she had, as she said, hardly " booed an ee," and every day her lonely sorrow was becoming truly " too deep for tears." The unexpected visit of even Jock Hall had helped for a moment to cause a reaction and to take her out of herself; and now that she perceived beyond doubt, what she was slow hitherto to believe, that her husband " wasna himsel' "—nay, that even *she* was strange to him, and was addressed by him in accents and with expressions betokening irritation towards her, and with words which were, for the first time, wanting in love, she became bewildered, and felt as if God had indeed sent her a terrible chastisement. It was fortunate that Hall had called—for neither her arguments nor her strength could avail on the present occasion. She immediately summoned Jock to her assistance. He was already behind her, for he had quickly cast off his boots, and approached the bed softly and gently, on perceiving the Sergeant's state. With a strong hand he laid the Sergeant back on his pillow, saying, "Ye will gang to the kirk, Sergeant, but I maun tell ye something afore ye gang. Ye'll mind Jock Hall? him that ye gied the boots to? An' ye'll mind Mr. Spence the keeper? I hae got an erran' frae him for you. He said ye wad be glad tae hear aboot him."

The Sergeant stared at Jock with a half-excited, half-stupid gaze. But the chain of his associations had for a moment been broken, and he was quiet as a child, the bells ringing no more as he paused to hear about his old friend Spence.

Jock's first experiment at nursing had proved successful. He was permitted, therefore, for that night only, as Katie said, to occupy the loft, to which he brought his straw bed and straw bolster; and his presence proved, more than once during the night, an invaluable aid.

The Doctor called next morning. Among his other causes for anxiety, one, and not the least, had been the impossibility of finding a respectable nurse. He was therefore not a little astonished to discover Jock Hall, the "ne'er-do-weel," well dressed, and attending the Sergeant. He did not at first ask any explanations of so unexpected a phenomenon, but at once admitted that he was better than none. But before leaving, and after questioning Jock, and studying his whole demeanour, and, moreover, after hearing something about him from Mrs. Mercer, he smiled and said, "Keep him by all means—I think I can answer for him;" and muttering to himself—"Peculiar temperament—hysterical, but curable with diet—a character—will take fancies—seems fond of the Sergeant—contagious fever—we shall try him by all means."

"Don't drink?" he abruptly asked Jock.

"Like a beast," Jock replied; "for a beast drinks jist when he needs it, Doctor, and sae div I; but I dinna need it noo, and winna need it, I think, a' my days."

"You'll do," said the Doctor; and so Jock was officially appointed to be Adam's nurse.

Adam Mercer lay many weary days with the fever heavy upon him—like a ship lying to in a hurricane, when the only question is, which will last longest, the storm or the ship? Those who have watched beside a lingering case of fever can alone comprehend the effect which intense anxiety, during a few weeks only, caused by the hourly conflict of "hopes and fears that kindle hope, an undistinguishable throng," produces on the whole nervous system.

Katie was brought into deep waters. She had never taken it home to herself that Adam might die. Their life had hitherto been quiet and even, —so like, so very like, was day to day, that no storm was anticipated to disturb the blessed calm. And now at the prospect of losing him, and being left alone in the wide, wide wilderness, without her companion and guide; her earthly all —in spite of the unearthly links of faith and love that bound them—lost to her, no one who has thus suffered will wonder that her whole flesh shrunk as from the approach of a terrible enemy. Then it was that old truths lying in her heart were summoned to her aid, to become practical powers in this her hour of need. She recalled all she had learned as to God's ends in sending affliction, with the corresponding duties of a Christian in receiving it. She was made to realise in her experience the gulf which separates *knowing* from *being* and *doing*—the right theory from the right practice. And thus it was that during a night of watching she fought a great battle in her soul between her own will and God's will, in her endeavour to say, not with her lips, for that was easy, but from her heart, "Thy will be done!" Often did she exclaim to herself, "Na, God forgie me, but I *canna* say 't!" and as often resolved, that "say 't she wad, or dee." At early morn, when she opened the shutters, after this long mental struggle, and saw the golden dawn spreading its effulgence of glory along the

eastern sky, steeping the clouds with splendours
of every hue from the rising sun of heaven, himself as yet unseen ; and heard the birds salute his
coming—the piping thrush and blackbird beginning their morning hymn of praise with the lark
"singing like an angel in the clouds"—a gush of
holy love and confidence filled her heart, as if
through earth and sky she heard the echo of her
Father's name. Meekly losing herself in the
universal peace, she sank down on her knees,
beside the old arm-chair, and with a flood of
quiet tears that eased her burning heart, she said,
"Father ! Thy will be done !"

In a short time she rose with such a feeling of
peace and freedom as she had never hitherto
experienced in her best and happiest hours. A
great weight of care seemed lifted off as if by
some mighty hand ; and though she dared not

affirm that she was now prepared for whatever might happen, she had yet an assured confidence in the goodness of One who *would* prepare her when the time came, and whose grace would be sufficient for her in any hour of need.

The interest felt by the parish generally, on the Sergeant's dangerous state becoming known, was great and sincere. In the presence of his sufferings, with which all could more or less sympathise — whether from their personal experience of sorrow, from family bereavements, or from the consciousness of their own liability to be at any moment visited with dangerous sickness— his real or supposed failings were for the time covered with a mantle of charity. It was not for them to strike a sorely wounded man.

Alas! for one that will rejoice with those who rejoice, many will weep with those who weep.

Sympathy with another's joy is always an unselfish feeling; but pity only for another's suffering may but express the condescension of pride towards dependent weakness.

But it is neither gracious nor comforting to scrutinise too narrowly the motives which influence human nature in its mixture of good and evil, its weakness and strength. We know that we cannot stand such microscopic examination ourselves, and ought not, therefore, to apply it to others. Enough that much real sympathy was felt for Adam. Some of its manifestations at an earlier stage of his illness were alluded to by Miss Thomasina in her conversation with Mr. Smellie. It was true that Mrs. Gordon had called in her carriage, and that repeatedly, to inquire for him—a fact which greatly impressed those in the neighbourhood who had treated him as a man far beneath them. Mr. Gordon, too, had been unremitting in quiet attentions; and Mrs. Mercer was greatly softened, and her heart delivered from its hard thoughts of many of her old acquaintances, by the kind and constant inquiries which day by day were made for her husband. Little Mary had to act as a sort of daily bulletin as she opened the door to reply to those who "speered for the Sergeant;" but no one entered the dwelling, from the natural fears entertained by all of the fever.

Many, too, spoke well of the Sergeant when he was "despaired of," who would have been silent respecting his merits had he been in health. Others also, no doubt, would have waxed eloquent about him after his burial. But would it not be well if those who act on the principle of saying all that is good about the dead, were to spend some portion of their charity upon the living? Their *post-mortem* store would not be diminished by such previous expenditure. No doubt it is "better late than never;" but would it not be still better if never so late? Perhaps not! So far as the good man himself is concerned, it may be as well that the world should not learn, nor praise him for, the many premiums he has paid day by day for the good of posterity until these are returned, like an insurance policy, in gratitude after he is screwed down in his coffin.

# CHAPTER XIII.

BUT what was the minister thinking about during the Sergeant's illness? Miss Thomasina had told him what had taken place during her interview with Smellie. Mr. Porteous could not comprehend the sudden revolution in the mind of his elder. But his own resolution was as yet unshaken; for there is a glory often experienced by some men when placed in circumstances where they stand alone, that of recognising themselves as being thereby sufferers for conscience sake—as being above all earthly influences, and firm, consistent, fearless, true to their principles, when others prove weak, cowardly, or compromising.  Doubts and difficulties, from whatever source they come, are then looked upon as so many temptations; and the repeated resistance of them, as so many evidences of unswerving loyalty to truth.

"I can never yield one jot of my principles," Mr. Porteous said to Miss Thomasina.  "The Sergeant ought to acknowledge his sin before the Kirk Session, before I can in consistency be reconciled to him!"  And yet all this sturdy profession was in no small degree occasioned by the intrusion of better thoughts, which because they rebuked him were unpleasant.  His irritation measured on the whole very fairly his disbelief in the thorough soundness of his own position, and made him more willing than he had any idea of to be reconciled to Adam.

We need not report the conversation which immediately after this took place in the Manse between Smellie and Mr. Porteous. The draper was calm, smiling, and circumspect. He repeated all he had said to Miss Thomasina as to the necessity and advantage of leniency, forgiveness, and mercy; dwelling on the Sergeant's sufferings and the sympathy of the parish with him; the noble testimony which the minister had already borne to truth and principle, and urged Mr. Porteous to gratify the Kirk Session by letting the case "tak' end;" but all his pleadings were apparently in vain. The minister was not verily "given to change!" The case, he said, had been settled by the Session, and the Session alone could deal with it. They were at perfect liberty to reconsider the question as put by Mr. Smellie, and which he had perfect liberty to bring before the court. For himself he would act as principle and consistency dictated. And so Smellie returned to his room above the shop, and went to bed, wishing he had left the Sergeant and his bird to their own devices ; and Mr. Porteous retired to his room above the study with very much the same feelings.

In the meantime one duty was clear to Mr. Porteous, and that was to visit the Sergeant. He was made aware of the highly contagious character of the fever, but this only quickened his resolution to minister as far as possible to the sick man and his family. He was not a man to flinch from what he saw to be his duty. Cowardice was not among his weaknesses. It would be unjust not to say that he was too real, too decided, too stern for that. Yielding to feelings of any kind, whether from fear of consequences to himself, physically, socially, or ecclesiastically,

was not his habit. He did not suspect—nor
would he perhaps have been pleased with the
discovery had he made it—that there was in
him a softer portion of his being by which he
could be influenced, and which could, in favourable circumstances, dominate over him. There
were in him, as in every man, holy instincts,
stronger than his strongest logic, though they
had not been cultivated so carefully. He had
been disposed rather to attribute any mere *sense*
or feeling of what was right or wrong to his
carnal human nature, and to rely on some
clearly defined rule either precisely revealed in
Scripture, or given in ecclesiastical law, for his
guidance. But that door into his being which
he had often barred as if against an enemy could
nevertheless be forced open by the hand of love,
that love itself might enter in and take possession.

Mr. Porteous had many mingled thoughts as one Saturday evening—in spite of his " preparations "—he knocked, at the cottage door. As usual, it was opened by Mary. Recognising the minister, she went to summon Mrs. Mercer from the Sergeant's room ; while Mr. Porteous entered, and, standing with his back to the kitchen fire, once more gazed at the starling, who again returned his gaze as calmly as on the memorable morning when they were first introduced.

Mrs. Mercer did not appear immediately, as she was disrobing herself of some of her nursing-gear—her flannel cap and large shawl—and making herself more tidy. When she emerged from the room, from which no sound came save an occasional heavy sigh, and mutterings from Adam, in his distress, her hair was dishevelled, her face pale, her step tottering, and years seemed to have been added to her age. Her eyes had no tear to dim their earnest and half-abstracted gaze. This visit of the minister, which she instinctively interpreted as one of sympathy and good-will—how could it be else?—at once surprised and delighted her. It was like a sudden burst of sunshine, which began to thaw her heart, and also to brighten the future. She sat down beside Mr. Porteous, who had advanced to meet her; and holding his proffered hand with a firm grasp, she gazed into his face with a look of silent but unutterable sorrow. He turned his face away. "Oh! sir," at last she said, "God bless you!—God bless you for comin'! I'm lanely, lanely, and my heart is like tae break. It's kind, kind o' ye, this;" and still holding his hand, while she covered her eyes with her apron as she rocked to and fro in the anguish of her spirit; "the loss," she said, "o' my wee pet was sair—ye ken what it was tae us baith," and she looked at the empty cot opposite, "when ye used tae sit here, and he was lyin' there—but oh! it was naething tae this, naething tae this misfortun'!"

The minister was not prepared for such a welcome, nor for such indications of unbounded confidence on Katie's part, her words revealing her heart, which poured itself out. He had expected to find her much displeased with him, even proud and sullen, and had prepared in his own mind a quiet pastoral rebuke for her want of meekness and submissiveness to Providence and to himself.

"Be comforted, Mrs. Mercer! It is the Lord! He alone, not man, can aid," said Mr. Porteous kindly, and feelingly returning the pressure of her hand.

Katie gently withdrew her hand from his, as if she felt that she was taking too great a liberty, and as if for a moment the cloud of the last few weeks had returned and shadowed her confidence in his good-will to her. The minister, too, could not at once dismiss a feeling of awkwardness from his mind, though he sincerely wished to do so. He had seldom come into immediate contact, and never in circumstances like the present, with such simple and unfeigned sorrow. Love began to knock at the door!

"Oh, sir," she said, "ye little ken hoo Adam respeckit and lo'ed ye. He never, never booed his knee at the chair ye're sittin' on wi'oot prayin' for a blessin' on yersel', on yer wark, an' on yer preaching. I'm sure, if ye had only heard him the last time he cam' frae the kirk "—

the minister recollected that this was after Adam's deposition by the Session—"hoo he wrastled for the grace o' God tae be wi' ye, it wad hae dune yer heart guid, and greatly encouraged ye. Forgie me, forgie me for sayin' this: but eh, he was, and is, a precious man tae me; tho' he'll no' be lang wi' us noo, I fear!" And Katie, without weeping, again rocked to and fro.

"He is a good man," he replied; "yes, a very good man is Adam; and I pray God his life may be spared."

"O thank ye, thank ye!" said Katie. "Ay, pray God his life may be spared—and mine too, for I'll no' survive him; I canna do't! nae mair could wee Mary!"

Mary was all the while eagerly listening at the door, which was not quite closed, and as she heard those words and the low cry from her "mother" beseeching the minister to pray, she ran out, and falling down before him, with muffled sobs hid her face in the folds of his great-coat, and said, " Oh, minister, dinna let faither dee! dinna let him dee!" And she clasped and clapped the knees of him who she thought had mysterious power with God.

The minister lifted up the agonised child, patted her fondly on the head, and then gazed on her thin but sweet face. She was pale from her self-denying labours in the sick room.

"Ye maun excuse the bairn," said Katie, "for she haesna been oot o' the hoose except for an errand sin' Adam grew ill. I canna get her tae sleep or eat as she used to do—she's sae fond o' the guidman. I'm awfu' behadden till her. Come here, my wee wifie." And Katie pressed the child's head and tearful face to her bosom, where Mary's sobs were smothered in a large brown shawl. "She's no' strong, but extraordinar' speerity," continued Katie in a low voice and apologetically to Mr. Porteous; "and ye maun just excuse us baith."

"I think," said the minister, in a tremulous voice, "it would be good for us all to engage in prayer."

They did so.

Just as they rose from their knees, the slight noise which the movement occasioned—for hitherto the conversation had been conducted in whispers, caused the starling to leap up on his perch. Then with clear accents, that rung over the silent house, he said, "I'm Charlie's bairn!"

Katie looked up to the cage, and for the first time in her life felt something akin to downright anger at the bird. His words seemed to her to be a most unseasonable interruption—a text for a dispute—a reminiscence of what she did not wish then to have recalled.

"Whisht, ye impudent cratur!" she exclaimed; adding, as if to correct his rudeness, "ye'll disturb yer maister."

The bird looked down at her with his head askance, and scratched it as if puzzled and asking "What's wrong?"

"Oh," said Katie, turning to the minister as if caught in some delinquency, "it's no' my faut, sir; ye maun forgie the bird; the silly thing doesna ken better."

"Never mind, never mind," said Mr. Porteous, kindly, "it's but a trifle, and not worthy of our notice at such a solemn moment; it must not distract our minds from higher things."

"I'm muckle obleeged to ye, sir," said Katie,

rising and making a curtsy.   Feeling, however, that a crisis had come from which she could not escape if she would, she bid Mary "gang ben and watch, and shut the door." When Mary had obeyed, she turned to Mr. Porteous and said, "Ye maun excuse me, sir, but I canna thole ye to be angry aboot the bird.   It's been a sore affliction, I do assure you, sir."

"Pray say nothing more of that business, I implore you, Mrs. Mercer, just now," said Mr. Porteous, looking uneasy, but putting his hand kindly on her arm ; "there is no need for it."

This did not deter Katie from uttering what was now oppressing her heart more than ever, but rather encouraged her to go on.

"Ye maun let me speak, or I'll brust," she said.   "Oh, sir, it has indeed been an awfu' grief this—just awfu' tae us baith.   But dinna, dinna

think Adam was to blame as muckle as me.
I'm in faut, no' him. It wasna frae want o'
respec' tae you, sir; na, na, that couldna be; but
a' frae love tae our bairn, that was sae uncommon
ta'en up wi' yersel'."

"I remember the lovely boy well," said Mr.
Porteous, not wishing to open up the question of
the Sergeant's conduct.

"Naebody that ever see'd him," continued
Katie, "but wad mind him—his bonnie een like
blabs o' dew, and his bit mooth that was sae
sweet tae kiss. An' ye mind the nicht he dee'd,
hoo he clapped yer head when ye were prayin'
there at his bedside, and hoo he said his ain
wee prayer; and hoo——" Here Katie rose in
rather an excited manner, and opened a press,
and taking from it several articles, approached
the minister and said—"See, there's his shoon,

and there's his frock ; and this is the clean cap and frills that was on his bonnie head when he lay a corp ; and that was the whistle he had when he signed tae the bird tae come for a bit o' his piece ; and it was the last thing he did, when he couldna eat, to insist on me giein' a wee bit tae his bairn, as he ca'ed it, ye ken ; and he grat when he was sae waik that he couldna whistle till 't. O, my bairn, my bonnie bairn ! " she went on, in low accents of profound sorrow, as she returned to the press these small memorials of a too cherished grief.

"You must not mourn as those who have no hope, my friend," said the minister; "your dear child is with Jesus."

"Thank ye, sir, for that," said Katie; who resolved, however, to press towards the point she had in view. " An' it was me hindered Adam frae killin' my bairn's pet," she continued, resuming her seat beside the minister. "He said he wad throttle it, or cast it into the fire."

The minister shook his head, remarking, " Tut, tut! that would never have done! No human being wished that."

"That's what I said," continued Katie; "an' whan he rowed up the sleeves o' his sark, and took haud o' the bit thing tae thraw its neck I wadna let him, but daured him to do it, that did I; and I ken't ye wad hae dune the same, fur the sake o' wee Charlie, that was sae fond o' you. O forgie me, forgie him, if I was wrang! A mither's feelings are no easy hauden doon!"

Was this account the truth, the whole truth, and nothing but the truth? Perhaps not. But then, good brother or sister, if you are disposed to blame Katie, we defend not even this weary mourner from thee. Take the first stone and cast it at her! Yet we think, as you do so, we see the Perfect One writing on the ground; and if He is writing her condemnation, 'tis in the dust of earth, and the kindly rain or winds of heaven will soon obliterate the record.

"No more about this painful affair, I beseech of you," said the minister, taking a very large and long pinch of snuff; "let us rather try and comfort Adam. This is our present duty."

"God Himsel' bless ye!" said Katie, kissing the back of his hand; "but ye maunna gang near him; dinna risk yer valuable life; the fivver is awfu' smittal. Dr. Scott wull let nae-body in."

"And have you no nurse?" inquired Mr. Porteous, not thinking of himself.

This question recalled to her mind what seemed

another mysterious stumbling-block. She knew not what to say in reply. Jock Hall was at that moment seated like a statue beside the bed, and what would the minister think when he saw this representative of parish wickedness in an elder's house?

She had no time for lengthened explanations; all she said, therefore, was, "The only nurse Dr. Scott and me could get was nae doot a puir bodie, yet awfu' strang and fit tae haud Adam doon, whan aside himsel'; and he had nae fear o' his ain life—and was a gratefu' cratur—and had ta'en a great notion o' Adam, and is kin' o' reformed—that—that I thocht—weel, I maun jist confess, the nurse is Jock Hall!"

"Jock Hall!" exclaimed the minister, lifting his eyebrows with an expression of astonishment; "is it possible? But I leave to you and

the Doctor the selection of a nurse. It is a
secular matter, with which officially I have
nothing to do. My business is with spiritual
things; let me therefore see the Sergeant. I
have no fear. I'm in God's hands. All I have
to do is my duty. That is my principle."

"Jist let me ben a minute first," asked Katie.

She went accordingly to the room and whispered to Jock, "Gang to the laft; the minister
is comin' ben.—Aff!"

"Mind what ye're baith aboot!" said Jock,
pointing to his patient. "Be canny wi' him—
be canny—nae preachin' e'enoo, mind, or flytin',
or ye'll rue 't. Losh, I'll no stan't!"

As the minister entered the room he saw
Jock Hall rapidly vanishing like a spectre, as he
stole to his den among the straw.

Mr. Porteous stood beside the Sergeant's bed,

and Katie said to her husband, bending over him—

"This is the minister, Adam, come tae see you, my bonnie man."

"God bless you and give you His peace!" said Mr. Porteous, in a low voice, drawing near the bed as Katie retired from it.

The Sergeant opened his eyes, and slowly turned his head, breathing hard, and gazing with a vacant stare at his pastor.

"Do you know me, Adam?" asked the minister.

The Sergeant gave the military salute and replied, "We are all ready, Captain! Lead! we follow! and, please God, to victory!"

He was evidently in the "current of the heady fight," and in his delirious dreams fancied that he was once more one of a forlorn hope about

to advance to the horrors of the breach of a be-
leaguered city, or to mount the ladder to scale
its walls. Closing his eyes and clasping his
hands, he added with a solemn voice, "And
now, my God, enable me to do my duty! I
put my trust in thee! If I die, remember my
mother. Amen. Advance, men! Up! Steady!"

The minister did not move or speak for a few
seconds, and then said, "It is peace, my friend,
not war. It is your own minister who is speaking
to you."

Suddenly the Sergeant started and looked
upward with an open, excited eye, as if he saw
something. A smile played over his features.
Then in a tone of voice tremulous with emotion, and with his arms stretched upwards as if
towards some object, he said, "My boy—my
darling! You there! Oh, yes. I'm coming to you.

Quick, comrades!  Up!"  A moment's silence,
and then if possible a steadier gaze, with a look
of rapture.  "Oh, my wee Charlie!  I hear ye!
Is the starling leevin'?  Ay, ay—that it is!  I
didna kill't!  Hoo could ye think that?  It was
dear to you, my pet, an'—"  Then covering his
face with his hands he said, "Oh! whatna licht
is that?  I canna thole't, it's sae bricht!  It's
like the Son o' man!"

He fell back exhausted into what seemed an
almost unconscious state.

"He's gane—he's gane!" exclaimed Katie.

"He's no' gane! gie him the brandy!" said
Jock, as he slipped rapidly into the room from
the kitchen; for Jock was too anxious to be
far away.  In an instant he had measured out
the prescribed quantity of brandy and milk in
a spoon, and, lifting the Sergeant's head, he

said, "Tak' it, and drink the king's health. The day is oors!" The Sergeant obeyed as if he was a child; and then whispering to Katie, Jock said, "The doctor telt ye, wumman, to keep him quaet; tak' care what ye're aboot!" and then he slipped again out of the room.

The Sergeant returned to his old state of quiet repose.

Mr. Porteous stood beside the bed in silence, which was broken by his seizing the fevered hand of the Sergeant, saying fervently, "God bless and preserve you, dear friend!" Then turning to Mrs. Mercer, he motioned her to accompany him to the kitchen. But for a few seconds he gazed out of the window blowing his nose. At length, turning round and addressing her, he said, "Be assured that I feel deeply for you. Do not distrust me. Let me only add that if Mary *must* be taken out of the house for a time to escape infection, as I am disposed to think she should be, I will take her to the Manse, if I cannot find another place for her as good as this —which would be difficult."

" Oh, Mr. Porteous ! I maun thank ye for ——"

" Not a word, not a word of thanks, Mrs. Mercer," interrupted the minister ; " it is my duty. But rely on my friendship for you and yours. The Lord has smitten, and it is for us to bear ;" and shaking her hand cordially, he left the house.

" God's ways are not our ways," said Katie to herself, "and He kens hoo to mak' a way o' escape out o' every trial."

Love ceased to knock for an entrance into the minister's heart; for the door was open and love had entered, bringing in its own light and peace.

# CHAPTER XIV.

A S the minister walked along the street, with the old umbrella, his inseparable companion in all kinds of weather, wet or dry, under his arm, and with his head rather bent as if in thought, he was met by Mrs. Craigie, who suddenly darted out—for she had been watching his coming—from the "close" in which she lived, and curtsied humbly before him.

"Beg pardon, sir," she said, "it's a fine day—I houp ye're weel. Ye'll excuse me, sir."

"What is it? what is it?" asked Mr. Porteous, in rather a sharp tone of voice, disliking the interruption at such a time from such a person.

"Weel," she said, cracking her fingers as if in a puzzle, "I just thocht if my dear wee Mary was in ony danger frae the fivver at the Sergeant's, I wad be willint—oo ay, real willint—for freendship's sake, ye ken, tae tak' her back tae mysel'"

"Very possibly you would," replied Mr. Porteous, drily; "but my decided opinion at present is, that in all probability she won't need your kindness."

"Thank ye, sir," said the meek Craigie, whose expression need not be analysed as she looked after Mr. Porteous, passing on with his usual step to Mr. Smellie's shop.

No sooner had he entered the "mercantile establishment" of this distinguished draper, than with a nod he asked its worthy master to follow him up to the sanctum. The boy was charged to let no one interrupt them.

When both were seated in the confidential retreat,—the scene of many a small parish plot and plan,—Mr. Porteous said, " I have just come from visiting our friend, Adam Mercer."

" Indeed ! " replied Smellie, as he looked rather anxious and drew his chair away. " I'm tellt the fever is maist dangerous and deadly."

" Are *you* afraid ?  An elder ?  Mr. Smellie ! "

" Me! I'm not frightened," replied the elder, drawing his chair back to its former position near the minister. " I wasn't thinking what I was doing. How did ye find the worthy man ? for worthy he is, in spite o' his great fauts—in fact, I might say, his sins."

" I need not, Mr. Smellie," said Mr. Porteous, " now tell you all I heard and witnessed, but I may say in general that I was touched—very much touched by the sight of that home of deep sorrow. Poor people!" and Mr. Porteous seemed disposed to fall into a reverie.

If there is anything which can touch the heart and draw it forth into brotherly sympathy towards one who has from any cause been an object of suspicion or dislike, it is the coming into personal contact with him when suffering from causes beyond his will. The sense is awakened of the presence of a higher power dealing with him, and thus averting our arm if disposed to strike. Who dare smite one thus in the hands of God? It kindles in us a feeling of our own dependence on the same omnipotent Power, and quickens the consciousness of our own deserts were we dealt with according to our sins. There is in all affliction a shadow of the cross, which must harden or soften—lead us upward or drag us downward. If it awakens the feeling of pity only in those who in pride stand afar off, it opens up the life-springs of sympathy in those who from good-will draw nigh.

Mr. Smellie was so far off from the Sergeant that he had neither pity nor sympathy: the minister's better nature had been suddenly but deeply touched; and he now possessed both.

" I hope," said Smellie, "ye will condescend to adopt my plan of charity with him. Ye ken, sir, I aye stand by you. I recognise you as my teacher and guide, and it's not my part to lead, but to follow. Yet if ye *could* see—oh, if ye *could* see your way, in consistency, of course, with principle—ye understan', sir ?—to restore Adam afore he dees, I wad be unco' prood—I hope I do not offend. I'm for peace."

And if Adam should recover, Mr. Smellie, thy charity might induce him to think well of thee. Is that thy plan?

"The fever," said Mr. Porteous, with a sigh, " is strong. He is feeble."

"Maybe, then, it might be as well to say nothing about this business until, in Providence, it is determined whether he lives or dies?" inquired the elder.

Did he now think that if the Sergeant died he would be freed from all difficulty, as far as Adam was concerned? Ah, thou art an unstable because a double-minded man, Mr. Smellie!

"I have been thinking," Mr. Porteous went on to say, "that, as it is a principle of mine to meet as far as possible the wishes of my people—as far as *possible*, observe, that is, in consistency with higher principles—I am quite willing to meet *your* wishes, and those of the Session, should they agree with yours, and to recognise in the Sergeant's great affliction the hand of a chastening Providence, and as such to accept it. And instead, therefore, of our demanding, as we had a full right to do in our then imperfect knowledge of the case, any personal sacrifice on the part of the poor Sergeant—a sacrifice, moreover, which I now feel would be—— but we need not discuss again the painful question, or open it up ; it is so far *res judicata.* But if you feel yourself free at our first meeting of Session to move the withdrawal of the whole case, for the several reasons I have hinted at, and which I shall more fully explain to the Session, and if our friend Mr. Menzies is disposed to second your motion, I won't object."

Mr. Smellie was thankful, for reasons known

to the reader, to accept Mr. Porteous' sugges-
tion. He perceived at once how his being the
originator of such a well-attested and official
movement as was proposed, on behalf of the
Sergeant, would be such a testimonial in his
favour as would satisfy John Spence should the
Sergeant die; and also have the same good results with all parties, as far as his own personal
safety was concerned, should the Sergeant live.

With this understanding they parted.

Next day in church Mr. Porteous offered up
a very earnest prayer for " one of our members,
and an office-bearer of the congregation, who is
in great distress," adding the petition that his
invaluable life might be spared, and his wife
comforted in her great distress. One might hear
a pin fall while these words were being uttered ;
and never did the hearts of the congregation

respond with a truer "Amen" to their minister's supplications.

At the next meeting of Session, Mr. Smellie brought forward his motion in most becoming and feeling terms. Indeed, no man could have appeared more feeling, more humble, or more charitable. Mr. Menzies seconded the motion with real good-will. Mr. Porteous then rose and expressed his regret that duty, principle, and faithfulness to all parties had compelled him to act as he had hitherto done; but from the interview he had had with Mrs. Mercer, and the explanations she had given him,—from the scene of solemn and afflicting chastisement he had witnessed in the Sergeant's house, and from his desire always to meet, as far as possible, the wishes of the Kirk Session, he was disposed to recommend Mr. Smellie's motion to their most favourable consideration. He also added that his own feelings had been much touched by all he had seen and heard, and that it would be a gratification to himself to forget and forgive the past.

Let us not inquire whether Mr. Porteous was consistent with his former self, but be thankful rather if he was not. Harmony with the true implies discord with the false. Inconsistency with our past self, when in the wrong, is a condition of progress, and consistency with what is right can alone secure it.

The motion was received with equal surprise and pleasure by the minority. Mr. Gordon, in his own name, and in the name of those who had hitherto supported him, thanked their Moderator for the kind and Christian manner in which he had acted. All protests and appeals to the Presbytery were withdrawn, and a minute to that effect was prepared with care by the minister, in which his "principles" were not compromised, while his "feelings" were cordially expressed. And so the matter "took end" by the restoration of Adam to his position as an elder.

No one was happier at the conclusion come to by the Session than the watchmaker. He said:—that he took the leeberty o' just makin' a remark to the effect that he thocht they wad a' be the better o' what had happened; for it was his opinion that even the best Kirk coorts, like the best toon clocks, whiles gaed wrang. Stoor dried up the ile and stopped the wheels till they gaed ower slow and dreich, far ahint the richt time. An' sac it was that baith coorts and clocks were therefore a hantle the better o' bein' scoored. He was quite sure that the Session wad gang fine and smooth after this repair. He also thanked

the minister for his motion, without insinuating
that he had caused the dust, but rather giving
him credit for having cleared it away, and for
once more oiling the machine.   In this sense the
compliment was evidently understood, and accepted by Mr. Porteous.   Even the solemn Mr.
Smellie smiled graciously.

# CHAPTER XV.

IT would only weary the reader to give a narrative of the events which happened during the period of the Sergeant's tedious recovery. Dr. Scott watched by him many a night, feeling his pulse, and muttering to himself about the twitching of the muscles of the fingers, as indicating the state of the brain. Often did he warn Katie, when too hopeful, that "he was not yet out of the wood," and often encouraged her, when desponding, by assuring her that he "had seen brokener ships come to land." And just as the captain steers his ship in a hurricane, adjusting

VOL. II.                          P

every rag of sail, and directing her carefully by
the wind and compass, according to the laws of
storms, so did the Doctor guide his patient.
What a quantity of snuff he consumed during
those long and dreary days! What whisky
toddy —— No! he had not once taken a single
tumbler until the night when bending over the
Sergeant he heard the joyful question put by him,
" Is that you, Dr. Scott? What are you doing
here?" and when, almost kissing Katie, he said,
" He is oot o' the wood at last, thank God!"

"The Almighty bless you!" replied Katie, as
she, too, bent over her husband and heard him
once more in calmness and with love utter her
name, remarking, "This has surely been a lang
and sair fecht!" He then asked, " Hoo's wee
Mary? Is the bird leevin'?" Seeing Jock Hall at
his bedside, he looked at his wife as if questioning

whether he was not still under the influence of a delirious dream. Katie interpreting his look said, " It was Jock that nursed ye a' through." " I'm yer nurse yet, Sergeant," said Jock, " an' ye maun haud yer tongue and sleep." The Sergeant gazed around him, turned his face away, and shutting his eyes passed from silent prayer into refreshing sleep.

One evening soon after this, Adam pale and weak, was seated, propped up with pillows, in his old arm-chair, near the window in his kitchen. The birds and the streams were singing their old songs, and the trees were in full glory, bending under the rich foliage of July; white fleecy clouds were sailing across the blue expanse of the sky; the sun in the west was displaying its glory, ever varying since creation; and all was calm and peaceful in the heavens above, and, as far as man could see, on the earth beneath.

Jock Hall was seated beside Adam, looking up with a smile into his face, and saying little except such expressions of happiness as, " I'm real prood to see you this length, Sergeant! Ye're lookin' unco' braw! It's the wifie did it, and maybe the Doctor, wi' that by ordinar' lassock, wee Mary;—but keep in yer haun's, or ye'll get cauld and be as bad as ever." Jock never alluded to the noble part he himself had taken in the battle between life and death.

Katie was knitting on the other side of her husband. Why interpret her quiet thoughts of deepest peace? Little Mary sat on her chair by the fire.

This was the first day in which Adam, weak and tottering, had been brought, by the Doctor's advice, out of the sick room.

Mr. Porteous unexpectedly rapped at the door,

and on being admitted, gazed with a kindly expression on the group before him. Approaching them, he shook hands with each, not omitting even Jock Hall, and then sat down. After saying a few suitable words of comfort and of thanksgiving, he remarked, pointing to Jock, that "he was snatched as a brand from the burning." Jock, as he bent down, and counted his fingers, replied that the minister "wasna maybe far wrang. It was him that did it;" but added, as he pointed his thumb over his shoulder, "an' though he wasna frichted for the lowe, I'm thinkin' he maybe got his fingers burned takin' me oot o't."

"Eh, Mr. Porteous," said Katie, "ye dinna ken what the puir fallow has been tae us a' in our affliction! As lang as I leeve I'll never forget——"

"As sure's I'm leevin'," interrupted Jock, "I'll

rin oot the hoose if ye gang on that way. It's really makin' a fule o' a bodie." And Jock seemed thoroughly annoyed.

Katie only smiled, and looking at him, said, "Ye're a guid, kind cratur, Jock."

"Amen," said Adam.

After a minute of silence, Mr. Porteous cleared his throat and said, "I am glad to tell you, Mr. Mercer, that the Session have unanimously restored you to the office of Elder."

The Sergeant started, and looked puzzled and pained, as if remembering "a dream within a dream."

"Unanimously and heartily," continued Mr. Porteous, "and when you are better we shall talk over this business as friends, though it need never be mentioned more. Hitherto, in your weakness, I requested those who could have communicated the news to you not to do so, in case it might agitate you; besides, I wished to have the pleasure of telling it to you myself. I shall say no more, except that I give you full credit for acting up to your light, or, let me say, according to the feelings of your kind heart, which I respect. Let me give you the right hand of fellowship."

A few quiet drops trickled down Adam's pale cheek, as in silence he stretched out his feeble and trembling hand, accepting that of his minister. The minister grasped it cordially, and then gazed up to the roof, his shaggy eyebrows working up and down as if they were pumping tears out of his eyes, and sending them back again to his heart. Katie sat with covered face, not in sorrow as of yore, but in gratitude too deep for words.

"Will ye tak' a snuff, sir?" said Jock Hall, as

with flushed face he offered his tin box to the minister. "When I fish the Eastwater I'll sen' ye as bonnie a basketfu' as ever ye seed, for yer kindness to the Sergeant; and ye needna wunner muckle if ye see me in the kirk wi' him sune."

The starling, for some unaccountable reason, was hopping from spar to spar of his cage, as if leaping for a wager.

Mary, attracted by the bird, and supposing him to be hungry, mounted a chair, and noiselessly opened the door of the cage. But in her eagerness and suppressed excitement she forgot the food. As she descended for it, the starling found the door open, and stood at it for a moment bowing to the company. He then flew out, and, lighting on the shoulder of the Sergeant, looked round the happy group, fluttered his feathers, gazed on the minister steadily,

and uttered in his clearest tones, " I'm Charlie's
bairn—' A man's a man for a' that!'"

\*    \*    \*    \*    \*    \*

Perhaps some of the readers of this village
story, in their summer holidays, may have fished
the streams flowing through the wide domain
of Castle Bennock, under the guidance of the
sedate yet original under-keeper, John Hall;
and may have "put up" at the neat and
comfortable country inn, the " Bennock Arms,"
kept by John Spence and his comely wife Mary
Semple—the one working the farm, and the
other managing the house and her numerous
and happy family. If so, they cannot fail to
have noticed the glass case in the parlour,
inclosing a stuffed Starling, with this inscription
under it—

" I'm Charlie's Bairn."

LONDON:
R. CLAY, SON, AND TAYLOR, PRINTERS,
BREAD STREET HILL.

# WORKS BY NORMAN MACLEOD, D.D.,

ONE OF HER MAJESTY'S CHAPLAINS.

I.

Third Thousand, with Seventy Illustrations, small 4to. 14*s.*

## EASTWARD:

### TRAVELS IN EGYPT, PALESTINE, AND SYRIA.

" The most enjoyable book on the Holy Land we have ever read."—*Noncon-formist.*

" This handsome volume, though not a novel, is a novelty among books of travel. The genial, manly spirit of the author gives a human colouring to every scene, and keeps awake in us as we accompany him an increasing sympathy."—*Daily News.*

" We have derived much pleasure from the perusal of a narrative which is at times as serious as a minister can make anything, and occasionally as amusing as a genuine humorist can really be. Were we to search the country, we doubt whether such a genial travelling companion as Dr. Macleod could be found, and many will delight in travelling 'Eastward' with him. . . . . The general reader will probably learn more from Dr. Macleod's way of describing than he could from the most precise explanation of the scientific proser."—*Press.*

II.

Sixteenth Thousand, crown 8vo. cloth, 3*s.* 6*d.*

## THE EARNEST STUDENT:

### BEING MEMORIALS OF JOHN MACKINTOSH.

" Full of the most instructive materials, and admirably compiled, we are sure that a career of unusual popularity awaits it ; nor can any student peruse it without being quickened by its example of candour, assiduity, and happy self-consecration."—*Dr. James Hamilton in " Excelsior."*

III.

Tenth Thousand, crown 8vo. cloth, 3*s.* 6*d.*

## THE OLD LIEUTENANT AND HIS SON.

" We place ' The Old Lieutenant and his Son ' in the very first rank of religious fiction. It contains remarkable evidence of the author's great talent."—*Daily News.*

" Beyond any book that we know, this story of Norman Macleod's will tend to produce manly kindness and manly piety."—*The Patriot.*

IV.

Ninth Thousand, crown 8vo. 3*s.* 6*d.*

## PARISH PAPERS.

" There is nothing narrow in sentiment, tame in thought, or prosy in style in these papers. Each paper is small in compass, but big with noble thoughts. It is just such a book as we should expect from an author whose Christianity is that of the Gospels rather than creeds, whose teaching is that of a Christ-loving man rather than that of a professional preacher, and whose nature is royal and not menial in its faculties and instincts."—*Homilist.*

V.

Eleventh Thousand, with Illustrations, gilt extra, 3*s.* 6*d.*

## THE GOLD THREAD:

### A STORY FOR THE YOUNG.

" This is one of the prettiest as it is one of the best children's books in the language. Wherever there are children, if our advice is taken, there will be a 'Gold Thread.' "— *Caledonian Mercury.*

VI.

Thirty-fifth Thousand, 6*d.*

## WEE DAVIE.

" Fraught with the truest poetry, rich in divine philosophy, unapproachably the chief among productions of its class—this, and more, is the story of ' Wee Davie.' By all means let every family have a copy of Dr. Macleod's inimitable Christian tale, which is as powerful a preacher of the Gospel as we have ever encountered."—*Dublin Warder.*

# LIST OF BOOKS

# ALEXANDER STRAHAN.

---

2 Vols. demy 8vo. price 36s.

## Lives of Indian Officers,

Illustrative of the History of the Civil and Military Services of India.

By JOHN WILLIAM KAYE,

Author of "The History of the War in Afghanistan," &c. &c.

Fourth Edition, post 8vo. price 12s.

## The Reign of Law.

By the DUKE OF ARGYLL.

" A very able book, well adapted to meet that spirit of inquiry which is abroad, and which the increase of our knowledge of natural things stimulates so remarkably. It opens up many new lines of thought, and expresses many deep and suggestive truths. It is very readable; and there are few books in which a thoughtful person will find more that he will desire to remember."—*Times.*

" The question with which the Duke of Argyll deals is just the point which pious and practical minds find the most perplexing. And he takes up the mental position which alone can promise usefulness in the treatment of such a question." *Saturday Review.*

" The aim of this book is lofty, and requires not only a thorough familiarity with metaphysical and scientific subjects, but a breadth of thought, a freedom from prejudice, a general versatility and sympathetic quality of mind, and a power of clear exposition rare in all ages and in all countries. We have no hesitation in expressing an opinion that all these qualifications are to be recognised in the Duke of Argyll, and that his book is as unanswerable as it is attractive."—*Pall Mall Gazette.*

" This is a masterly book. It is the first from any Cabinet Minister of standing on the philosophy of science; and it shows, we think, almost as large a power of thought and as strong a judgment within its sphere as any of Sir Cornewall Lewis's books, and more than many of Mr. Gladstone's. . . . The book is strong, sound, mature, able thought from its first page to its last."—*Spectator.*

" A very remarkable volume, which must certainly have some good result in clearing the ground for the advance of truth."—*Examiner.*

" We have experienced the greatest delight in reading the ' Reign of Law.' That part of the work which relates to birds is as interesting as a fairy tale. The style of his Grace (to say nothing here of his thought, of which others have spoken words of admiration certainly not too strong) often runs into poetry; and it has everywhere that indescribable not-too-muchness which is always the *cachet* of high-class work."—*Illustrated Times.*

" A really valuable contribution to science, and conciliatory in the best sense of the term." — *Westminster Review.*

A

# WORKS BY SARAH TYTLER.

2 Vols. post 8vo. 21s.

## Days of Yore.

" Every quality of merit which was conspicuous in 'Citoyenne Jacqueline' is apparent here also. The first tales in these volumes give us some of the finest descriptions of scenery we have ever read, while the meditative mood into which Miss Tytler frequently falls in these eighteenth century reminiscences is very like the delightful chit-chat with which Thackeray indulged his readers so often."—*Spectator.*

"The concentrated power which we admire in 'Citoyenne Jacqueline' is precisely the kind of power to ensure an equal success to the author in ' Days of Yore.' No story in the book disappoints us : each has 'the virtue of a full draught in a few drops ;' and in each there is the quintessence of such a novel as Thackeray might have written."—*Pall Mall Gazette.*

Crown 8vo. 6s.

## Citoyenne Jacqueline :

### A Woman's Lot in the Great French Revolution.

"The characters stand out in marked individuality, living and breathing creatures, while the scenery is as delicately true to nature as if a Gainsborough or a Linnell had painted it. It is a charming book."—*Reader.*

" The author charms us immediately into keen interest in the scenes. and sympathy with the characters of her story. which shows a power of catching and reproducing to the life French piquancy and levity." — *Pall Mall Gazette.*

"A piece of more thorough and conscientious literary workmanship has rarely come before us. . . . The

dramatic representation of her personages is perfect."—*British Quarterly Review.*

" There is real genius in the book." —*Spectator.*

" ' Citoyenne Jacqueline ' is a daring and successful story ; it is powerfully dramatic, full of vivid contrast and rapid movement. . . . Its place will be among the highest of historical novels."—*Scotsman.*

" ' Citoyenne Jacqueline ' is one of those rare books of which every sentence deserves to be read leisurely. and will repay the attention with pleasure."—*Guardian.*

Crown 8vo. 5s.

## Papers for Thoughtful Girls.

" One of the most charming books of its class that we have ever read."— *Morning Herald.*

" One of the most fascinating books we have ever seen for the rising youth

of the fair sex. The whole volume is so lively and yet so serious, that we would disclaim all liking for the young lady who should not fall in love with it."—*Eclectic Review.*

Crown 8vo. 5s.

## The Diamond Rose :

### A Life of Love and Duty.

Crown 8vo. 5s.

## Fortunes and Misfortunes :

### The Story of some Endeavours after Happiness.

# WORKS BY C. J. VAUGHAN, D.D.
VICAR OF DONCASTER.

Small 8vo. 4s. 6d.

## Voices of the Prophets:
Or Faith, Prayer, and Holy Living.

Small 8vo. 4s. 6d.

## Plain Words on Christian Living.
### CONTENTS.

1. Sleep and Waking.
2. The Seat and Exit of Evil.
3. Temptation.
4. Conscience.
5. The Christian Use of Food.
6. The Christian Use of Society.
7. Domestic Service; (1) Masters and Servants.
8. Domestic Service; (2) Servants and Masters.
9. A Good Old Age.
10. Repentance and Forgiveness Once Needed.
11. Repentance and Forgiveness Occasionally Needed.
12. Repentance and Forgiveness Daily Needed.
13. Address for a Harvest Home.
14. The Decisive Question.
15. The Marks of the Lord Jesus.
16. The Revelation of the Unseen.

Small 8vo. 4s. 6d.

## Christ the Light of the World.
### CONTENTS.

1. Why He Came.
2. The Lamp and the Light.
3. Nunc Dimittis.
4. Uses of Light.
5. A Man of Sorrows.
6. The Gospel of the Fall.
7. The Gospel of the Flood.
8. Christ the Lord of Nature.
9. Christ the Conqueror of Satan.
10. Christ the Destroyer of Death.
11. Christ the Sinner's Friend.
12. Cast Out and Found.

Small 8vo. 4s. 6d.

## Characteristics of Christ's Teaching.
Drawn from the Sermon on the Mount.
### CONTENTS.

1. Who are Happy? First, Second, and Third Answers.
2. Who are Happy? Fourth Answer.
3. Who are Happy? Fifth Answer.
4. Who are Happy? Sixth Answer.
5. Who are Happy? Seventh Answer.
6. Who are Happy? Eighth and Last Answer.
7. What are Christians? Two Answers.
8. Christ interprets the Law: Five Examples.
9. Christ warns us against Three Counterfeits.
10. Christ teaches us the Manner of Prayer.
11. Of the Candle of the Soul, which is a Single Intention.
12. Christ teaches us what we ought to Seek: Two Things.
13. Christ warns us against Judging.
14. Christ counsels Discrimination.
15. The Charter of Prayer.
16. Christ points out to us the Gate of Life.
17. Concluding Cautions.

A 2

## WORKS BY HENRY ALFORD, D.D.
### DEAN OF CANTERBURY.

## The Year of Prayer;
Being Family Prayers for the Christian Year.

*There are Two Editions of this Book—one for Heads of Families, price 3s. 6d., and a smaller one for the other Members of the Household, price 1s. 6d.*

## The Year of Praise;
Being Hymns with Tunes, for the Sundays and Holidays of the Year, intended for use in Canterbury Cathedral, and adapted for Cathedral and Parish Churches generally.

Edited by HENRY ALFORD, D.D. Dean of Canterbury.
Assisted in the Musical Part by ROBERT HAKE, M.A. Precentor, and THOMAS EVANCE JONES, Organist, of Canterbury Cathedral.

*[In the Press.*

Small 8vo. 3s. 6d.

## How to Study the New Testament.
Section I.—The Gospels and the Acts of the Apostles.

Small 8vo. 3s. 6d.

## Eastertide Sermons.
Preached before the University of Cambridge on Four Sundays after Easter, 1866.

Small 8vo. 5s.

## The Queen's English.
Stray Notes on Speaking and Spelling.

"This volume ought to be well studied by writers and speakers."—*Morning Post.*

"A volume full of suggestive hints to speakers and writers."—*Guardian.*

Fourth Edition, containing many Pieces now first collected, small 8vo. 5s.

## The Poetical Works of Henry Alford.

Small 8vo. 5s.

## Meditations :
In Advent, on Creation, on Providence.

Crown 8vo. 7s. 6d.

## Letters from Abroad.

# WORKS BY DORA GREENWELL.

Small 8vo. *6s.*

# Essays.

Contents :—
1. Our Single Women—2. Hardened in Good—3. Prayer—
4. Popular Religious Literature—5. Christianos ad Leones.

" Miss Greenwell's Essays are very graceful, and are written with a real knowledge of their subjects. The book is really a good one. '—*Spectator.*
" We highly value all the Essays for their good sense, fine feeling, and hearty religiousness, and for the fresh-

ness and piquancy of their style. Together they form one of the most admirable pleas for, and defences of, Christian philanthropy which have lately issued from the press."—*Nonconformist.*

Enlarged Edition, small 8vo. *6s.*

# Poems.

"Here is a poet as true as George Herbert or Henry Vaughan or our own Cowper. We advise our readers to possess the book, and get the joy and the surprise of so much real thought and feeling. It is a cardiphonia set to music."—*North British Review.*
" Miss Greenwell is specially endowed as a writer of sacred poetry; and it is the rarest realm of all, with the fewest competitors for its crown. She seems to us to be peculiarly fitted

with natural gifts for entering into the chambers of the human heart, and to be spiritually endowed to walk there, with a brightening influence, cheering, soothing, exalting, with words of comfort and looks of love, as a kind of Florence Nightingale walking the hospital of ailing souls."—*Athenæum.*
" Amongst volumes of verse lately given to the world, none has truer and richer poetic qualities than this."—*Nonconformist.*

Small 8vo. *2s. 6d.*

# The Patience of Hope.

"This is the most thoughtful and suggestive book of our day."—*Witness.*
"A work of singular philosophic power, as well as poetic beauty."—*Family Treasury.*
" Our admiration of the searching,

fearless speculation, the wonderful power of speaking clearly upon dark and all but unspeakable subjects, the rich outcome of ' thoughts that wander through eternity,' increases every time we take up this wonderful little book."—*North British Review.*

Third Edition, small 8vo. *2s. 6d.*

# The Covenant of Life and Peace.

"The production of a thoughtful, cultivated Christian mind, setting forth, in great fulness and beauty, the

present privileges of the believer."
—*Baptist Magazine.*

Small 8vo. *3s. 6d.*

# Two Friends.

" We cannot read these pages without seeing that they are the production

of a thoughtful and earnest mind."—
*London Review.*

# WORKS BY EDWARD IRVING.

5 Volumes, demy 8vo. £3.

## The Collected Writings of Edward Irving.

Edited by his Nephew the Rev. G. CARLYLE, M.A.

*\*\* More than one-half of these Writings are now printed for the first time.*

"Edward Irving had the power of teaching the true sublime, and the English language can show no more magnificent specimens of religious eloquence than those that are contained in these Collected Writings."—*Times.*

"Irving, almost alone among recent men, lived his sermons and preached his life. His words, more than those of any other modern speaker, were 'life passed through the fire of thought.' He said out his inmost heart, and this it is that makes his writings read like a prolonged and ideal biography."—*The Saturday Review.*

"The greatest preacher the world has ever seen since apostolic times."—*Blackwood's Magazine.*

"Irving was the freest, brotherliest, bravest human soul mine ever came in contact with. I call him, on the whole, the best man I have ever, after trial enough, found in this world or now hope to find."—*Thomas Carlyle in Fraser's Magazine.*

Post 8vo. 6s.

## Miscellanies from the Collected Writings of Edward Irving.

"It is by such a volume as this, we are inclined to think, that Irving will come to be widely known to general readers. There are passages of a purely theological character which, we think, display profound wisdom, and are models of clear, strong, living utterance. There are practical and ethical 'sayings,' that are as gold and rubies and diamonds. We entirely approve the principle of its compilation, and welcome it as fitted, in a very remarkable manner, to quicken genuine and deep religious feeling, and to impart earnestness and force to the religious life."—*Nonconformist.*

3 vols. demy 8vo.

## The Prophetical Writings of Edward Irving. [In the Press.

# WORKS BY WILLIAM GILBERT.

2 vols. post 8vo. 21s.

## Doctor Austin's Guests.

"More than any other writer of fiction that we could name, Mr. Gilbert possesses the power of investing an imaginary narrative with the character of a plain, unvarnished statement of facts. In reading his pages one seems to be listening to a person who is not broaching theories or communicating impressions, but simply registering, in a sober and straightforward manner, matters that have fallen under his observation or within his actual experience. His realism is the realism of Balzac and Defoe. We congratulate Mr. Gilbert on having made a decided advance in his art. This work is better, we think, than any of his previous ones."— *Saturday Review.*

"Mr. Gilbert is one of our best story-tellers, and we cannot give much higher praise to 'Dr. Austin's Guests' than to say that it is quite as clever a book as 'Shirley Hall.' It is individual. No other known writer could have written such a book so well."— *Examiner.*

"We give this book no slight praise when we say that it is worthy of Defoe."— *Westminster Review.*

Crown 8vo. Illustrated, 5s.

## The Magic Mirror.

### A Round of Tales for Old and Young.

"The stories are well told in the best style for children, and the little woodcuts to illustrate them have the merit of showing an unhackneyed mode of treatment."—*The Times.*

"This is such a book as Nathaniel Hawthorne alone could have written."—*New York Round Table.*

Crown 8vo. 6s.

## De Profundis :

### A Tale of the Social Deposits.

"Mr. Gilbert's novels do more to enlarge the field of actual experience than those of any other writer of the day. . . . Defoe and Mr. Gilbert alone of English novelists seem to give the ore of English life, while other novelists of equal power give only the extracted metal. . . . We think 'De Profundis' the most powerful of Mr. Gilbert's powerful stories."—*Spectator.*

"A remarkably clever book."—*Athenæum.*

"We know of no book which will give so true an idea of the poor of London."—*Churchman.*

"He engraves with a pen of iron and the point of a diamond; his paintings are like the most unrelieved of Millais'. They call to mind the picture of the 'Vale of Rest,' which held the eye by such a powerful fascination some years since in the Exhibition of the Academy: and we most heartily thank Mr. Gilbert for this, which, while no doubt his most successful, seems to be also his most purposeful book."—*The Eclectic.*

"Mr. Gilbert has a dramatic faculty which many professed dramatists might well envy, and a purity of style which, in his department of literature, has only been surpassed by Defoe."—*Nonconformist.*

Square 16mo. Illustrated, 2s. 6d.

## The Washerwoman's Foundling.

# WORKS BY ROBERT BUCHANAN.

Small 8vo. 5s.

## London Poems.

"A series of life-like character-pictures. If Mr. Buchanan writes no more, he will have permanently enriched English literature by what he has already accomplished."—*British Quarterly Review.*

"There is something very graceful in every one of these dozen 'London Idyls,' and it is the grace of thorough completeness and proportion—the sound mind in the sound body—so far superior to any mere polish or trick of style. Several are exquisitely touching."—*Church and State Review.*

"We hardly know of any narrative poetry greater than is found in some of these sad and mourning lines. . . . These verses have been lived before they were written down."—*Athenæum.*

"No volume has appeared for many years in London which so certainly announces a poetic fame."—*Spectator.*

"As a poet combining simplicity with pathos and a wonderful talent for giving to his subjects the forms of reality and life Mr. Buchanan is unsurpassed. Among contemporaries and recent writers he is unequalled."—*Court Circular.*

"They are in their subject so pathetic—so repelling, one might almost say; in their realism so pre-Raphaelite; and yet in their poetic treatment so delicately and tenderly artistic ; that one cannot choose but wonder and admire, and be sad over them."—*Morning Star.*

Small 8vo. 5s.

## Idyls and Legends of Inverburn.

"Mr. Buchanan is a man of original genius ; such faculty as he has is independent, individual. And if we look closely into his poems we shall be struck with the fact that, although quite free from mannerism or eccentricity, which would call attention to any marked peculiarity isolating him from contemporaries, his thought and style are distinctively his own. He has none of the showy graces which make inconsiderate readers exclaim, 'How clever, how poetical !' While reading the poems you never think of the poet. It is only in the afterglow of emotion you think of him, and then

you know what rare power was needed to produce so genuine an effect."—Art. "Robert Buchanan," by G. H. Lewes, in the *Fortnightly Review.*

"One of the most charming volumes of poetic narrative that we know."—*Pall Mall Gazette.*

"We do not call to mind any volume of modern poetry so rich in tenderly told story, beautifully painted picture, and abundant, spontaneous music."—*Illustrated Times.*

"One who can write thus has a claim to be considered a true poet and master of hearts."—*Eclectic Review.*

Small 8vo. 5s.

## Undertones.

"The offspring of a true poet's heart and brain, they are full of imagination, fancy, thought, and feeling ; of subtle perception of beauty, and harmonious expression."—*Daily News.*

"Poetry, and of a noble kind."—*Athenæum.*

"Great intelligence, fine workman-

ship, and dramatic power almost unexampled in this half century."—*Illustrated Times.*

"It is life from within that in these pages invests the ancient myths with fresh meaning and beauty. Yet luxuriance of descriptive power there is too."—*Scotsman.*

# WORKS BY THOMAS GUTHRIE, D.D.

### EDITOR OF THE SUNDAY MAGAZINE.

Crown 8vo. 3s. 6d.

## Our Father's Business.

Crown 8vo. 3s. 6d.

## Out of Harness.

#### CONTENTS.

The Edinburgh Original Ragged School.
New Brighton.
A Winter Gale.
The Streets of Paris.
Sunday in Paris and French Protestantism.
Sketches of the Cowgate :—
  I. Dr. Chalmers and the Cowgate.
  II. Old Houses and Old Inscriptions.

III. The Blind Organist.
IV. The Orphan.
V. The Convict.
VI. Evangelistic Efforts.
Winter.
Autumn.
The Pest, Providence, and Prayer.
Watch-Night.
The Rechabites.
Unforgiving and Unforgiven.

Crown 8vo. 3s. 6d.

## Man and the Gospel.

"In point of striking thought, as well as apposite and beautiful illustration, this work will stand comparison with any which bears its author's name. The subjects of which it treats are as varied as they are interesting, and belong to that class which, as Lord Bacon says, 'come home to men's business and bosoms.'"—*Edinburgh Courant.*

Crown 8vo. 3s. 6d.

## The Parables

### Read in the Light of the Present Day.

"No one can so fittingly explain the Parables of the New Testament as Dr. Guthrie. He is a master of imagery, who scarcely writes a sentence without a comparison, and who has, moreover, the no less essential qualities of clear spiritual insight and strong, shrewd sense."—*Freeman.*

Crown 8vo. 3s. 6d.

## Speaking to the Heart.

"Dr. Guthrie never speaks without speaking to the heart; but these discourses bear with unwonted vividness the impress of his great emotional nature. They glow, they sparkle, they burn with intense feeling. We have seldom looked into a more fascinating book."—*English Churchman.*

32mo. 1s. 6d.

## The Angels' Song.

"A charming little book on some of the most interesting and important topics connected with human redemption. The style is glowing and brilliant, and the tone throughout is that of fervent and unwavering faith."—*Journal of Sacred Literature.*

## WORKS BY E. H. PLUMPTRE, M.A.

PROFESSOR OF DIVINITY, AND CHAPLAIN, KING'S COLLEGE, LONDON.

Popular Edition, crown 8vo. price 7s. 6d.

# The Tragedies of Sophocles :

### A New Translation, with a Biographical Essay.

"Let us say at once that Professor Plumptre has not only surpassed the previous translators of Sophocles, but has produced a work of singular merit, not less remarkable for its felicity than its fidelity ; a really readable and enjoyable version of the old plays."—*Pall Mall Gazette.*

Small 8vo. 5s.

# Lazarus and Other Poems.

"Professor Plumptre's freshness and originality of thought in treating familiar subjects give a great charm to what we may term his Biblical Idyls." *Churchman.*

"The volume cannot fail to establish Mr. Plumptre's reputation as a devotional poet of a high order of merit."—*Morning Post.*

Small 8vo. 5s.

# Master and Scholar, and other Poems.

"The present volume will certainly add to Professor Plumptre's reputation. It is worthy to be put on the same shelf with Heber and his own favourite Keble."—*Westminster Review.*

Small 8vo. 6s.

# Theology and Life.

"There is a degree of freshness and of originality about Mr. Plumptre's sermons which is wanting in a large majority of discourses. They contain the ring of true metal, and are of intrinsic value, independently of their suitableness to the immediate purpose of their delivery."—*Press.*

Demy 8vo. price 12s.

# Christ and Christendom ;

### Being the Boyle Lectures for 1866.

"A learned, thoughtful, and candid book, able in a literary sense, catholic in tone and spirit, full of the minute study and special knowledge of a life devoted to divinity, and one which will, for many minds, throw fresh light on the subtler and less conspicuous coincidences of the Gospel history."—*Spectator.*

"One of the most valuable and unanswerable defences of Christianity that have lately appeared."—*London Review.*

8vo. sewed, 6d.

# Sunday.

"A learned, comprehensive, and singularly candid and valuable treatise."—*Scotsman.*

# WORKS BY ALEXANDER SMITH.

Crown 8vo. 6s. with Coloured Frontispiece.

## A Summer in Skye.

"Mr. Smith has great command of language. Every page displays ingenious expressions, highly wrought comparisons, minute descriptions. 'A Summer in Skye' is to us very interesting indeed."—*Saturday Review.*

"With the exception of Mr. Ruskin and Mr. Kingsley, we should be puzzled where to go amongst living authors for better word-painting."—*Reader.*

"There are passages in the present volume which show the author's marvellous power of reproducing at will the magnificent effects of mountain scenery—passages in which a play of fancy and a true poetic insight strongly reinforce an illustration already presented with great facility of expression and rich colouring."—*Nonconformist.*

"Mr. Alexander Smith speaks of Boswell's Journal as 'delicious reading:' his own work, though after a very different fashion, affords delicious reading also. His egotism is never offensive; it is very often charming. If the traveller is sometimes lost in the essayist, who will not prefer an Elia to a Pennant?"—*Daily News.*

Crown 8vo. 3s. 6d.

## Dreamthorp:

### A Book of Essays written in the Country.

". . . A book to be read in the spirit of lazy leisure, to the sound of bubbling brooks and whispering woods. It is exquisitely printed, handy, handsome, and cheap."—*Athenæum.*

2 vols. small 8vo. 12s.

## Alfred Hagart's Household.

"The author paints with the most ordinary colours, but he has Opie's receipt for mixing them 'with brains.' It is his skill not only in selecting the most attractive and suggestive traits of character, but in expressing them in the most graceful and suggestive language, that gives unusual interest o 'Alfred Hagart's Household.' The author has the poet's power of translating tersely what he interprets from nature, of condensing vague feelings into tangible and graceful shape, and of mirroring by a simile what description would render inadequately. . . . Mr. Smith invests the simplest everyday characters and incidents with a freshness and grace which charm us."—*Pall Mall Gazette.*

"It is a sort of prose idyl, as dramatic in its details as 'Hermann and Dorothea.'"—*Athenæum.*

"We want novelists with a touch of poetry in them. We want novelists whose love of the poetic will preserve them from sensational absurdities. Such a novelist we find in Mr. Smith."—*Press.*

"No one can read 'Alfred Hagart's Household' without a sense of keen enjoyment."—*Guardian.*

## WORKS BY A. K. H. B.

Crown 8vo. 3s. 6d.

# The Recreations of a Country Parson.

"It is impossible not to be pleased with the 'Recreations of a Country Parson,' or to feel otherwise than on the best possible terms with the author."—*Saturday Review.*

"These delightful papers are full of the best qualities of the best essayists: they show close observation, clear insight, wit, humour, fancy, feeling, and humanity."—*Inverness Courier.*

Crown 8vo. 3s. 6d.

# The Graver Thoughts of a Country Parson.

"Many of them are exquisite essays on the subjects of which they treat; and in all there is a clearness and a simplicity, combined with the evidence of an original genius, which cannot fail to delight and instruct the reader."—*Morning Post.*

"Charming specimens of the Country Parson's Graver Thoughts. There is a fragrance like that of 'incense-breathing morn' on every page."—*Baptist Magazine.*

Crown 8vo. 3s. 6d.

# Counsel and Comfort,

### Spoken from a City Pulpit.

"Here there is evident heart-work —an earnestness that ought ever to be apparent in those seeking to guide, counsel, and comfort. We have perused the volume with pleasure, and so commend it to the notice of our readers, certain they will endorse our opinion as to its merits."—*Saturday Post.*
"The book is not sermons, but

essays, highly characteristic both for their thinking and their style. Originality, blended with genius, is apparent throughout. The reading is that of which the thoughtful man will never tire; and the book is such that they who have read it once will read it again."—*Christian Witness.*

# WORKS BY JOHN DE LIEFDE.

2 Volumes, post 8vo. Illustrated, 22s.

# Six Months among the Charities of Europe.

This Work describes, among other representative charities on the Continent, the large establishments devoted to the care of the Indigent, the Blind, the Fatherless, the Aged Poor, the Neglected Women and Children, and the Discharged Prisoners.

"The many thousands of English readers who are ready at home to take part in such works, and who would know, by faithful and pleasant report, what has been achieved elsewhere by the beneficent energies of earnest men and women, will find in this book a full body of the most pertinent information, full of encouragement and good suggestions."—*Examiner.*

"Mr. de Liefde's book is readable, interesting, stimulating. It shows how moral energy will overcome obstacles that seem enormous, how faith and enthusiasm move mountains."—*Fortnightly Review.*

"The author's method is especially valuable to all those who have to manage institutions of the kind."—*Globe.*

"This book is excellent. It will be eagerly read by persons of practical benevolence. It shows how much can be done by determination and singleness of purpose to diminish the sum of human suffering, and to promote the happiness of mankind. The author writes conscientiously of what he has observed, and gathers together an immense amount of experience and history relating to various kinds of charities. Such a work cannot fail to be extensively appreciated."—*Daily News.*

Small 8vo. Illustrated, 3s. 6d.

# The Postman's Bag.

## A Story-Book for Boys and Girls.

"This little volume is simple, artless, and Christian. We know several little children who are never weary of these stories, and we are sure that they can learn from them nothing but what is good."—*London Review.*

"Commend us to Mr. De Liefde for a pleasant story, whether in the parlour or on the printed page. He is himself a story-book, full of infectious humour, racy anecdote, youthful freshness, and warm-hearted religion. In this pretty little volume we do not get any of his more elaborate tales; it is professedly a book 'for boys and girls,' and is made up of short stories and fables, the very things to win children's hearts."—*Patriot.*

Crown 8vo. 5s.

# The Romance of Charity.

Being an Account of some Remarkable Institutions on the Continent.

Crown 8vo.

# Truth in Tales.

[*In the Press.*

# WORKS BY HORACE BUSHNELL, D.D.

Crown 8vo. 7s. 6d.

## The Vicarious Sacrifice,

### Grounded on Principles of Universal Obligation.

"This work is an important contribution to theological literature, whether we regard the amount of thought which it contains, the systematic nature of the treatise, or the practical effect of its teaching. No one can rise from its study without having his mind enlarged by its profound speculation, his devotion stirred by its piety, and his faith established on a broader basis of thought and knowledge."—*Guardian.*

Crown 8vo. 3s. 6d.

## Nature and the Supernatural,

### As Together constituting the One System of God.

"It is a work of great ability, and full of thought which is at once true and ingenious."—*Edinburgh Review.*

Crown 8vo. 6s.

## Christ and His Salvation,

### In Sermons variously related thereto.

"These sermons are distinguished from the ordinary discourses of the pulpit by being the product not merely of religious faith and feeling, but of religious genius."—*Atlantic Monthly.*

Crown 8vo. 3s. 6d.

## The New Life.

"We have here a Christian preacher dealing with some of the profoundest themes of Christian experience, with an insight into the working of the human soul, a grasp and breadth of thought, and a depth of experience, such as we have never seen equalled. The soul of the reader of this volume comes into vital contact with another soul which has reflected deep on life's great problems, has suffered in life's struggles, and found a healing balm in Christ's works, and repose in communion with God."—*Patriot.*

Crown 8vo. 6s.

## Christian Nurture;

### Or the Godly Upbringing of Children.

"The thinking is original, vigorous, and suggestive. The book is one that cannot be read without profit and pleasure of no transient character."—*Montrose Standard.*

Crown 8vo. 3s. 6d.

## Work and Play.

"This book is a collection of papers on general subjects, treated in a religious spirit. To say that they are worthy of the writer is sufficient recommendation."—*Baptist Magazine.*

# BY GEORGE MACDONALD, M.A.

Crown 8vo. price 5s.

## Unspoken Sermons.

"True and beautiful thought. musically and eloquently expressed." — *Pall Mall Gazette.*

"Readers will rejoice over these sermons as those who have gotten great spoil."—*Nonconformist.*

"'Unspoken Sermons,' by George MacDonald, bring us to the feet of a very charming preacher. We do not acquiesce in some of his theology; and there are sentiments in this volume to which we must take exception. But in George MacDonald's company the very air seems impreg-nated with love, purity, and tenderness. We seem to be under an Italian sky; and the harshness, whether of individual or national temperament, is wonderfully checked. A loving heart reveals to us the heart which is the fountain of love, and sends us away ashamed of our harsh and bitter feelings and praying to be able to love more both Him who is Love and those who ought ever to be dear to us for His sake."—*Dr. Guthrie's "Sunday Magazine."*

Square 16mo. 2s. 6d., Illustrated by ARTHUR HUGHES.

## Dealings with the Fairies.

Popular Edition, crown 8vo. cloth, 6s.

## Annals of a Quiet Neighbourhood.

"It is as full of music as was Prospero's island; rich in strains that take the ear captive and linger long upon it."—*Saturday Review.*

"A true and noble work."—*Daily News.*

"Whoever reads this story once will read it many times. It shows an almost supernatural insight into the workings of the human heart."—*Pall Mall Gazette.*

"This story is one that only a man of genius could have written."—*Examiner.*

# BY ALEXANDER VINET.

Post 8vo. 8s.

## Outlines of Theology.

Post 8vo. 8s.

## Outlines of Philosophy and Literature.

"These volumes are of great merit and extreme interest. The editor, M. Astie, has done his work with remarkable skill, and has succeeded in giving us a remarkable embodiment of M Vinet's thinking on the several sub-jects that pass under review. . . . Our readers will find in them a rich vein of vigorous thought, extremely suggestive, and always pervaded by a devout and reverent spirit."—*British Quarterly Review.*

# BOOKS FOR WORKING PEOPLE.

Seventy-second Thousand, crown 8vo. boards, 1s. 6d.

## Better Days for Working People.
By WILLIAM G. BLAIKIE, D.D. F.R.S.E.

Fifth Thousand, crown 8vo. cloth, 3s. 6d.

## Heads and Hands in the World of Labour.
By WILLIAM G. BLAIKIE, D.D. F.R.S.E.

Crown 8vo. boards, 1s. 6d.

## Counsel and Cheer for the Battle of Life.
By WILLIAM G. BLAIKIE, D.D. F.R.S.E.

Crown 8vo. boards, 1s. 6d.

## The Representation and Education of the People.
Lectures delivered at the Working Men's College.
By FREDERICK DENISON MAURICE, M.A.

Small 8vo. cloth, 2s. 6d.

## Simple Truth spoken to Working People.
By NORMAN MACLEOD, D.D. One of Her Majesty's Chaplains.

Small 8vo. sewed, 6d.

## Plain Words on Health.
Lay Sermons to Working People.
By JOHN BROWN, M.D.

Small crown 8vo. 2s. 6d.

## Progress of the Working Classes from 1832 to 1867.
By J. M. LUDLOW and LLOYD JONES.

A Popular Book for Ministers, Teachers, Students, and
Bible Readers generally.

In crown 8vo. 700 pages, price 6s. Volumes I. & II. of

# The Critical English Testament,

Being an Adaptation of Bengel's Gnomon, with numerous Notes,
showing the Precise Results of Modern Criticism and Exegesis.

Edited by Rev. W. L. BLACKLEY, M.A. and Rev. JAMES
HAWES, M.A.

The Publisher is desirous of drawing attention to this important
work, the purpose of which is to enable the English reader, with
the Authorized Version in his hand, and without any knowledge of
Greek, to understand the precise results of modern criticism in
revising the text of the New Testament. It seems strange that the
English language has been until now without a book containing
this information.

"Of Bengel's 'Gnomon,' Archdea-
con Hare justly said—'He condenses
more matter into a line than can be
extracted from pages of other writers.'
The 'Gnomon' still stands *facile prin-
ceps;* it needs supplementing, but it
has not been superseded. Such sup-
plement the editors have supplied by
incorporating the most important results of modern textual criticism, such
as are contained in the works of Tischendorf, Alford, Ellicott, and others.
A more valuable handbook for the
Bible student could not have been
supplied."—*British Quarterly Review.*

"The Editors of this valuable work
have put before the English reader the
results of the labours of more than
twenty eminent commentators. He
who uses the book will find that he is
reading Bengel's suggestive 'Gnomon,'
modifying it by the critical investiga-
tions of Tischendorf and Alford, and
comparing it with the exegetical notes
of De Wette, Meyer, Olshausen, and
others, and adding to it also profound
remarks and glowing sayings from the
writings of such men as Trench and
Stier."—*Evangelical Magazine.*

\*\*\* The Critical English Testament will be completed in three
volumes, averaging 700 pages each. Books of this class are, as a
rule, high-priced, and adapted to the few rather than to the many.
But the Publisher means this Book to be an exception, and has
accordingly fixed the price at 6s. a volume.

*Now Ready*—Vol. I. THE GOSPELS.

    ,,    —Vol. II. THE ACTS AND THE PASTORAL EPISTLES.

*In Preparation*—Vol. III. THE OTHER EPISTLES AND THE APO-
CALYPSE.

B

## DEVOTIONAL AND RELIGIOUS BOOKS.

Cloth antique, 1s. 6d.

# Personal Piety:
A Help to Christians to Walk worthy of their Calling.

Cloth antique, 1s. 6d.

# The Sunday Evening Book for Family Reading.

Cloth antique, 1s. 6d.

# Aids to Prayer.

Small 8vo. cloth antique, 3s. 6d.

# Christian Companionship for Retired Hours.

Small 8vo. 3s. 6d.

# Conversion.
By the Rev. ADOLPH SAPHIR.

Small 8vo. 1s. 6d.

# The Higher Christian Life.
By the Rev. W. E. BOARDMAN.

Small 8vo. 1s. 6d.

# The Way Home.
By the Rev. CHARLES BULLOCK.

Small 8vo. 1s.

# Blind Bartimeus, and his Great Physician.
By the Rev. W. G. HOGE.

Cheap Edition, sewed, 4d.

# The Still Hour.
By AUSTIN PHELPS.

Small 8vo. 2s. 6d.

# Man's Renewal.
By AUSTIN PHELPS, Author of "The Still Hour."

# BOOKS FOR THE YOUNG.

Square 16mo. Illustrated, 1s. 6d.

## The Will-o'-the-Wisps are in Town;
And other New Tales.
By HANS CHRISTIAN ANDERSEN.

Square 16mo. Illustrated, 2s. 6d.

## Edwin's Fairing.
By EDWARD MONRO, M.A.

Square 16mo. Illustrated, 2s. 6d.

## Æsop's Fables.

Square 16mo. Illustrated, 2s. 6d.

## Lilliput Levee:
Poems of Childhood, Child-fancy, and Child-like Moods.

Square 8vo. Illustrated, 3s. 6d.

## Wordsworth's Poems for the Young.

Square 16mo. Illustrated, 3s. 6d.

## Stories told to a Child,
By the Author of "Studies for Stories."

Small 8vo. Illustrated, 3s. 6d.

## The Postman's Bag.
By JOHN DE LIEFDE.

Square 8vo. Illustrated, 3s. 6d.

## The Gold Thread.
By NORMAN MACLEOD, D.D.

Crown 8vo. Illustrated, 5s.

## The Magic Mirror.
By WILLIAM GILBERT.

Square 16mo. Illustrated, 2s. 6d.

## The Washerwoman's Foundling.
By WILLIAM GILBERT.

B 2

Crown 8vo. 3s. 6d.

# The Treasure-book of Devotional Reading.

### Edited by BENJAMIN ORME, M.A.

"This is a beautiful book, but its contents are even better than their accompaniment. Such a book, we feel, is not to be criticised save by one who should miss many of his favourite authors. But this is not likely to be the case."—*Spectator.*

"We willingly bear witness to the beauty and soundness of the selected passages."—*Record.*

"It is the best book of the kind that we know of."—*Clerical Journal.*

"A volume rich in beauty and in unction, appealing at once to the taste and the heart."—*Freeman.*

"A beautiful volume, which never fails to offer something pleasant and profitable to the reader, wherever it is opened."—*London Quarterly Review.*

"A really valuable selection."—*Literary Churchman.*

"The selection is a good one."—*Pall Mall Gazette.*

"The selections have been made with care, and will be prized not merely as something to be read in an idle hour, but to be pondered over."—*Literary Churchman.*

Cloth antique, 1s. 6d.

# The Pathway of Promise.

Small 8vo. 2s. 6d.

# Able to Save;

### Or, Encouragement to Patient Waiting.

By the Author of "The Pathway of Promise."

Small 8vo. 2s. 6d.

# The Throne of Grace.

By the Author of "The Pathway of Promise."

Sewed, 6d.

# Address to his Parishioners.

By the Author of "The Pathway of Promise."

Crown 8vo. 3s. 6d.   Pocket Edition, small 8vo. 2s.

# Praying and Working.

By the Rev. W. FLEMING STEVENSON.

"The story of the lives of noble and devoted men. . . . This record of men's faith in God's help will be read with interest and sympathy, for it touches the electric chain with which we are darkly bound."—*Athenæum*.

Crown 8vo. 3s. 6d.

# Beginning Life.

By the Rev. PRINCIPAL TULLOCH.

"An excellent book for young men."—*Edinburgh Review*.

Crown 8vo. Illustrated, 6s.

# Studies for Stories from Girls' Lives.

"Simple in style, warm with human affection, and written in faultless English, these five stories are studies for the artist, sermons for the thoughtful, and a rare source of delight for all who can find pleasure in really good works of prose fiction. . . . They are prose poems."—*Athenæum*.

"Each of these studies is a drama in itself, illustrative of the operation of some particular passion—such as envy, misplaced ambition, sentimentalism, indolence, jealousy. In all of them the actors are young girls, and we cannot imagine a better book for young ladies."—*Pall Mall Gazette*.

"There could not be a better book to put into the hands of young ladies."—*Spectator*.

Crown 8vo. 2s. 6d.

# The Words of the Angels ;

Or, their Visits to the Earth, and the Messages they delivered.

By RUDOLPH STIER, D.D.

"'The Words of the Angels' is full of just and beautiful thought. Each narrative of angelic communication is carefully and beautifully expounded, and its meaning and lessons pointed out. The book is one with which every devout reader will be charmed."—*Patriot*.

Crown 8vo. cloth, 3s. 6d.

# Christian Believing and Living.

By F. D. HUNTINGDON, D.D.

Small 8vo. 5s.

# The Restoration of the Jews :

The History, Principles, and Bearings of the Question.

By DAVID BROWN, D.D. Author of "The Second Advent."

Post 8vo. 6s.

# The Philosophy of the Conditioned:

### Sir WILLIAM HAMILTON and JOHN STUART MILL.

### By the Rev. HENRY LONGUEVILLE MANSEL, D.D. Oxford.

"This volume is distinguished by the same clearness of style, cogency of argument, accuracy of information, and mastery of the subjects, which characterise all the other valuable productions of the author, and is on the points criticised a most successful as well as a most unsparing exposure of Mill's manifold errors."—*British Quarterly Review.*

Second Edition, with Additions, 2 vols. 14s.

# Henry Holbeach:

### Student in Life and Philosophy.

A Narrative and a Discussion. With Letters to Mr. Matthew Arnold, Mr. Alexander Bain, Mr. Thomas Carlyle, Mr. Arthur Helps, Mr. G. H. Lewes, Rev. H. L. Mansel, Rev. F. D. Maurice, Mr. John Stuart Mill, and Rev. Dr. J. H. Newman.

"Mr. Holbeach's volumes have remarkable merits."—*Athenæum.*

"The brave manner in which mere utilitarianism, materialism, positivism, and authority are grappled with, convinces the reader that he is in the hands of one who has read extensively and thought profoundly on all the terrible questions of the day."—*British Quarterly Review.*

"The author seems to be a man of sweet and serious mind, quick to be moved by great ideas, and with native affinities with what is delicate and exquisite. The book is one which will speak pleasantly to the cultivated reader."—*Pall Mall Gazette.*

"In the picture of the obscure Puritan colony there are touches worthy of George Eliot."—*Spectator.*

"We have never been more puzzled than in the attempt to give our readers a just idea of this remarkable book."—*Guardian.*

Demy 8vo. 7s. 6d.

# Ecclesia Dei:

The Place and Functions of the Church in the Divine Order of the Universe, and its Relations with the World.

"These thoughtful views on 'the Place and Functions of the Church in the Divine Order of the Universe, and its Relations with the World,' have a charm of language and method that render them exceedingly attractive... In the Appendix, the author unfolds a scheme for the revival of Church Life; and to this, as well as to the most suggestive matter that precedes it, we invite the attention of our readers."—*Spectator.*

"This is a very remarkable work, the execution of a grandly conceived theory... We fully expect to find that its intrinsic and literary excellence will soon force a way into public notoriety, and secure a due appreciation."—*John Bull.*

Crown 8vo. 2s. 6d.

# Church Life:

### Its Grounds and Obligations.

### By the Author of "Ecclesia Dei."

Crown 8vo. 6s.

# Familiar Lectures on Scientific Subjects.

By Sir JOHN F. W. HERSCHEL, Bart.

"A book of most profound and romantic scientific charm. . . . Without any strain of manner, the author paints picture after picture from the wonderful discoveries made known to us by the study of the physical forces at work on the earth and in the heavens."—*Spectator.*

Crown 8vo. Illustrated, 6s.

# God's Glory in the Heavens.

By WILLIAM LEITCH, D.D. Late Principal of Queen's College, Canada.

"We cannot conclude our notice of Dr. Leitch's book without dwelling upon the admirable manner in which the astronomical facts contained in it are blended with practical observa- tions and the highest and most enno- bling sentiments. It is thus that books on popular science should ever be written."—*The Reader.*

With Thirty-six Illustrations by the Author, printed in Colours by Leighton Brothers. Crown 8vo. 9s.

# A Year at the Shore.

A Companion Book for the Sea-side.

By PHILIP HENRY GOSSE, F.R.S.

"A delicious book deliciously illustrated."—*Illustrated London News.*

Small 8vo. Illustrated, 6s. People's Edition, crown 8vo. Fancy Covers, 1s.

# The Autocrat of the Breakfast-table.

By OLIVER WENDELL HOLMES.

Square 8vo. With Photographs and Plates, 12s.

# Our Inheritance in the Great Pyramid.

By Professor C. PIAZZI SMYTH, F.R.SS.L. and E., Astronomer Royal for Scotland.

"We commend Professor Smyth's very fascinating, paradoxical, and truly Christian book on 'Our Inheritance in the Great Pyramid' to all lovers of genuine goodness, of stubborn mathe- matics, and of adventurous theoriz- ing."—*London Quarterly Review.*

Crown 8vo. 6s.

# Views and Opinions.

By MATTHEW BROWNE.

"Mr. Matthew Browne's volume of essays is the work of a highly sensitive and cultivated mind. There is a rare and original vein of sportive humour running throughout its pages. . . . These are rare qualities; and the book in which they are displayed has few if any recent equals."—*Westminster Re- view.*

Small 8vo. cloth, 5s.

# Duchess Agnes, etc.

### By Isa Craig.

"A book of verse which will certainly give Miss Craig a place among the sisterhood of living singers."—*Athenæum.*

Crown 8vo. 3s. 6d.

# The Near and the Heavenly Horizons.

### By the Countess de Gasparin.

"This is a charming book. The Countess de Gasparin has the touch of genius which has the strange gift of speaking to everyone 'in their own tongue.'"—*Athenæum.*

Small 8vo. 5s.

# Human Sadness.

### By the Countess de Gasparin.

"There are times when the soul craves an utterance for its deeper longings. The Countess de Gasparin has given expression to these desires, and has done so in beautiful and affecting language."—*London Review.*

Small 8vo. 3s. 6d.

# The Higher Education of Women.

### By Emily Davies.

"There is so much temperance, good sense, and originality in Miss Davies' treatment of the question that it would be a most regrettable thing if she failed to ensure a wide circle of readers."—*Westminster Review.*

Small 8vo. 4s.

# Essays on Woman's Work.

### By Bessie Rayner Parkes.

"Every woman ought to read Miss Parkes's little volume on Woman's Work."—*Times.*

Second Thousand, crown 8vo. 6s.

# Vignettes :

### Twelve Biographical Sketches.

### By Bessie Rayner Parkes.

"This is a very charming volume. It will make many acquainted with persons worthy of being known, who have hitherto been names and nothing more."—*British Quarterly Review.*

Small 8vo. 5s.

# Woman's Work in the Church.

### Being Historical Notes on Deaconesses and Sisterhoods.

### By John Malcolm Ludlow.

"Of the importance of the subject of this book there can be no question, and Mr. Ludlow has brought to its discussion an intense sympathy, a large amount of information, and a calm, judicial spirit."—*British Quarterly Review.*

Third and Cheaper Edition, crown 8vo. with Portrait and
Woodcuts, 6s.

# Memoirs of the Life and Philanthropic Labours of Andrew Reed, D.D.

Prepared from Autobiographic Sources by his Sons, ANDREW
REED, B.A. and CHARLES REED, F.S.A.

"The sons of Andrew Reed have done a good work in publishing this memorial of their father."—*Athenæum.*

"A profoundly interesting piece of biography."—*Weekly Messenger.*

Crown 8vo. 3s. 6d.

# Story of the Lives of Carey, Marshman, and Ward.

By JOHN C. MARSHMAN.

Crown 8vo. 3s. 6d.

# My Ministerial Experiences.

By the Rev. Dr. BUCHSEL, Berlin.

"This is an interesting volume. It contains very interesting accounts of the German Pietists, amongst whom Dr. Buchsel was constantly known,

and who maintained the pure gospel in the midst of abounding Rationalism."—*Record.*

Post 8vo. 7s. 6d.

# Tangled Talk.

An Essayist's Holiday.

"'Tangled Talk' is the work of a true essayist. . . . It is a mosaic of suggestive bits ; or, since mosaic is a false image, let us say it is a skein of bright and broken threads, every one

of which may readily be woven into the reader's own thoughts, adding colour and strength to them for the future."—*Illustrated Times.*

Small 8vo. 1s. 6d.

# The Power of Prayer.

By the REV. Dr. PRIME.

Small 8vo. 1s. 6d.

# Prevailing Prayer.

With Introduction by NORMAN MACLEOD, D.D.

Post 8vo. 7s. 6d.

# " The Life and Light of Men."

By JOHN YOUNG, LL.D. (Edin.) Author of "The Christ of History."

"The author's idea is beautifully worked out in this volume, which, like all Dr. Young's writings, is characterised by deep thought and the keenest appreciation of spiritual things."—*Spectator*.

"As acute in argument as it is reverent in spirit."—*Clerical Journal*.

"Worked out with great skill and illustrated with considerable beauty."—*Patriot*.

Crown 8vo. 7s. 6d.

# Sermons and Expositions.

By the late JOHN ROBERTSON, D.D. Glasgow Cathedral.

"A noble man—a comprehensive scholar—a truly able Preacher."—*Eclectic*.

"Dr. Robertson had not a superior among the Scottish clergy ; for manly grasp of mind, for pith and point in treating his subject, he had hardly an equal. Let it be added that a more genial, kindly, liberal-minded and honest man never walked this earth."—*Fraser's Magazine*.

Crown 8vo. 6s.

# The Prophet Jonah :

His Mission and Character Illustrated and Applied.

By the Rev. HUGH MARTIN, M.A.

"It is impossible not to admire Mr. Martin's skill and boldness."—*British and Foreign Evangelical Review*.

"The work is both practical and expository, and will prove a valuable contribution to theological literature.

It is as well suited for general reading as for reference."—*London Review*.

"An acute and able exposition—marked by rare freshness and power."—*Sunday Magazine*.

Small 8vo. 6s.

# Personal Names in the Bible.

By the Rev. W. F. WILKINSON, M.A. Vicar of St. Werburgh's, Derby, and Joint Editor of "Webster and Wilkinson's Greek Testament."

"This is a book for all who would wisely, justly, and carefully study the sacred volume."—*Homilist*.

Crown 8vo. sewed, 1s.

# Romanism and Rationalism as opposed to Pure Christianity.

By JOHN CAIRNS, D.D.

Post 8vo. 10s. 6d.

# Lotta Schmidt,

And other Stories.

By ANTHONY TROLLOPE.

Post 8vo. 10s. 6d.

# Arne :

A Sketch of Norwegian Peasant Life.

By BJORNSTJERNE BJORNSON.

Translated by AUGUSTA PLESNER and SUSAN RUGELEY-POWERS.

"The most charming love-story of the year."—*Illustrated Times.*
"Such fresh little bits of nature come to us rarely. They are green spots in the arid waste of fiction."—*Athenæum.*
"It is, in fact, a fairy-book for men and women."—*Westminster Review.*

2 vols. post 8vo. 21s.

# Wealth and Welfare.

By JEREMIAH GOTTHELF.

"For a long time we have not read a book in which the style was at once so fresh and individual without being forced. The two volumes are a perfect little mine of shrewd observation."—*London Review.*

Demy 8vo. 7s. 6d.

# The Resources and Prospects of America.

Ascertained during a Visit to the States in the Autumn of 1865.

By Sir S. MORTON PETO, Bart. M.P.

"It deals entirely with the material and commercial capabilities of the country, and, as these are points on which it is almost impossible to take too sanguine a view, the book is likely to be equally acceptable on both sides of the Atlantic."—*Times*, April 12, 1866.

Small 8vo. Illustrated by Whymper, 5s.

# The Regular Swiss Round.

In Three Trips.

By the Rev. HARRY JONES, M.A.

2 vols. Demy 8vo. Illustrated, 21s.

# Cosas de España :

Illustrative of Spain and the Spaniards as they are.

By Mrs. WM. PITT BYRNE, Author of "Flemish Interiors," &c.

"The best book we have yet seen on Spain."—*Daily News.*

Crown 8vo. 5s.

# The Bible Student's Life of our Lord.

### By Rev. SAMUEL J. ANDREWS.

"For most readers this book will be far more interesting than any other work on our Lord's earthly life. It is written with great simplicity and in a deeply religious spirit; and it may with much advantage be placed in the hands, not of theological students only, but of all intelligent readers of the Bible."—*Contemporary Review.*

"Sensible, thorough, and impartial. It will be found very useful to divinity students."—*Guardian.*

Crown 8vo. 6s.

# The Foundations of our Faith.

### By Professors AUBERLEN, GESS, and others.

CONTENTS.

Introduction. By Prof. Riggenbach.
What is Faith? By Professor Riggenbach.
Nature or God. By Wolfgang Friedrich Gess.
Sin; its Nature and Consequences. By Ernest Stahelin.
The Old Testament Dispensation and the Heathen World. By Professor Auberlen.
The Person of Jesus Christ. By Professor Riggenbach.

Christ's Atonement for Sin. By Wolfgang Friedrich Gess.
The Resurrection and Ascension of Jesus Christ. By Professor Auberlen.
The Holy Spirit and the Christian Church. By S. Preiswerk.
The Doctrine of Justification by Faith. By Dr. Immanuel Stockmeyer.
The Future. By Ernest Stahelin.
Part I. The Immortality of the Soul.
Part II. Eternal Life.

"We know nothing that can compare with this work for completeness, Wisdom, and power."—*Nonconformist.*

Crown 8vo. 3s. 6d.

# Royal Truths.

### By HENRY WARD BEECHER.

". . . . To those who like a fresh dewy thought to lay upon their heart in the morning, or to lay upon a friend's heart, we heartily commend this vigorous and healthy book."—*Patriot.*

Crown 8vo. 3s. 6d.

# Eyes and Ears.

### By HENRY WARD BEECHER.

Crown 8vo. 2s. 6d.

# Life Thoughts.

### By HENRY WARD BEECHER.

"Here are 400 pages of the wisest, deepest, and most striking utterances, by one of the most original, brilliant, and versatile minds of the age."—*Baptist Quarterly.*

"A singularly fresh and suggestive book."—*Christian Treasury.*
"A most remarkable work." —*British Messenger.*

In Imperial 4to. price 21s.

# Touches of Nature.

### By Eminent Artists and Authors.

This Volume contains One Hundred Drawings on Wood, set in gold borders, and produced in the highest style of art, under the superintendence of Messrs. DALZIEL BROTHERS.

"This collection is one of the best that has ever appeared. It comprises drawings by Millais, Holman Hunt, Frederick Walker, Sandys, Wolf, Lawless, Du Maurier, Tenniel, Marcus Stone, Leitch, and half a dozen other men, more or less distinguished. Some of them are as good as can be found anywhere : Holman Hunt's drawing on p. 6 is an instance—a figure of a Jewish Reaper, which is beautiful beyond praise, a thing which demands and deserves contemplation as a masterly work of art. Besides Mr. Hunt, Mr. Millais and Mr. Walker are seen in this volume at their best, and so is Mr. Du Maurier."— *Pall Mall Gazette.*

"Millais's drawings here are all in his best style, and Mr. Holman Hunt's is perhaps the most remarkable in the collection. Mr. Sandys furnishes some very striking illustrations ; Mr. Wolf presents us with a collection of birds such as he alone can draw ; Mr. Linton a landscape, with one of those skies which he so much loves. We would gladly go on to specify others, but must content ourselves with briefly commending Mr. Small, Mr. Houghton, Mr. Walker, and especially Mr. Barnes ; and adding a word of deep regret for the loss of Mr. Paul Gray, whose pictures here show how true a lover of nature he was. But the chief value of the work is the testimony, which most certainly it bears, to the soundness and healthiness of English art in the present day. And it must be remembered that the illustrations were originally designed for 'Good Words,' the price of which is only 6d. ; but which fully deserves both its high reputation and wide circulation, by the spirit and good taste with which it is conducted."— *Westminster Review.*

Demy 4to. cloth gilt, 16s.

# Millais's Illustrations.

### A Collection of Drawings on Wood.

### By JOHN EVERETT MILLAIS, R.A.

"Foremost among the Illustrated Books deserves to be named Mr. Millais's 'Collected Illustrations.' Mr. Millais has qualities as an artist with which few authors can dare a comparison. What these qualities are may be inferred from the fact that here are his best illustrations collected together, separate from the text to which they belonged. They are works of art that need no letterpress —no comment : they speak for themselves, and have an interest by themselves. They nearly all display extraordinary power, and some of them are in their way quite perfect."— *Times.*

"A collection of the choicest drawings that have appeared in 'Good Words' and other finely illustrated periodicals, has been collected into one handsome volume. By the phrase 'choicest drawings' we mean—nor do we think that the fitness of that phrase, so applied, will be for a moment questioned—the drawings of Mr. John Everett Millais. If anybody wishes to see how a great artist will condescend to learn the mechanism of any subordinate branch of art in which he is called upon to work, there is no better source of information on the point than this book affords. The wood-cutter has been met, and all his modes of effect have been considered by the painter, so that a perfect union of their forces has been gained, to the incalculable advantage of popular art."— *Daily Telegraph.*

*" Good Words are worth much and cost little."*—HERBERT.

Sixpence Monthly, Illustrated.

# Good Words.

## Edited by NORMAN MACLEOD, D.D.

*And illustrated with Wood Engravings from designs by Millais, Holman Hunt, Keene, Walker, Wolf, Watson, and others.*

The experiment has now been tried of establishing a Magazine which should reflect the every-day life of a good man—with its times of religious thought and devotional feeling, naturally passing into other times of healthy recreation, busy work, intellectual study, poetic joy, or sunny laughter;—and its success has exceeded the most sanguine hopes of its projectors. "Good Words" was commenced seven years ago, and now enjoys a larger circulation than any other Monthly Magazine.

The following are among the Contributors to the Parts already published :—

Dean Alford.
Dean Alexander.
Duke of Argyll.
W. Lindsay Alexander, D.D.
A. K. H. B. Author of "The Recreations of a Country Parson."
Professor Ansted.
Rev. William Arnot.
Rev. William Arthur, A.M.
Author of "John Halifax."
Rev. Thomas Binney.
Professor J. S. Blackie.
Sir David Brewster, D.C.L.
John Brown, M.D.
Robert Buchanan.
John Caird, D.D.
Isa Craig.
Rev. J. Ll. Davies.
J. H. Merle D'Aubigné, D.D.
Principal Forbes.
The Countess De Gasparin.
Mrs. Gatty.
Archd. Geikie, F.G.S.
William Gilbert.
James Glaisher, F.R.S.
Mrs. Margaret Maria Gordon.
P. H. Gosse, F.R.S.
Dora Greenwell.
Thomas Guthrie, D.D.
James Hamilton, D.D.
John Hollingshead.
Sir John F. W. Herschel, Bart.
Jean Ingelow.
J. W. Kaye.

Rev. Charles Kingsley.
Rev. Professor Lee.
J. M. Ludlow.
Miss Marsh.
Gerald Massey.
Professor McCosh.
George MacDonald.
J. R. Macduff, D.D.
Norman Macleod, D.D.
Mrs. Oliphant.
Laurence Oliphant.
Rev. J. J. Stewart Perowne, D.D.
Professor Lyon Playfair.
Professor J. L. Porter.
Adelaide A. Procter.
Rev. Charles Pritchard, F.R.S.
Rev. W. Morley Punshon.
Rev. Professor Plumptre.
Henry Rogers.
Samuel Smiles.
Alexander Smith.
Professor C. Piazzi Smyth.
Dean Stanley.
W. Fleming Stevenson.
Isaac Taylor.
Sir W. Thomson.
Rev. A. W. Thorold.
Anthony Trollope.
Rev. Principal Tulloch.
Sarah Tytler.
C. J. Vaughan, D.D.
Archbishop Whately.
Catherine Winkworth.
Andrew Wynter, M.D.

The Volumes of "Good Words" are Elegantly Bound in Mauve Cloth extra, and Full Gilt, price 7s. 6d. each.

*⁎* *Each Year's Issue forms a Complete Book.*

The Back Volumes and Parts are always in print, and may be had by order of any Bookseller.

Sevenpence Monthly, Illustrated.

# The Sunday Magazine.

Edited by THOMAS GUTHRIE, D.D.

While aiming to bring the Bible into relation to common life, the "Sunday Magazine" seeks to express the devoutest thoughts of worship. Theology and the story of the Church; missions and missionaries; illustrations of God's glory in His works, and God's care in His providence; homilies on daily duties; and tales and sketches of character, all find a place. Human life has many relations, Christian experience many shades, the truth many sides : this Magazine addresses itself to each.

To make good our entry into cottages as well as drawing-rooms, to be read by people of all denominations, to be of no class, of no sect, of no party, but belonging to all and profitable to all—such is our aim. In brief, it is our desire to aid in calling off the mind from the secular objects which necessity forces upon it during the week ; to awaken from their torpor those feelings of gratitude and adoration which the Divine greatness and goodness should excite ; and to make the regular return of Sunday as healthful to society as the showers which soften, fertilize, and beautify the earth, bringing with them the influence of heaven.

The Volume commencing October, 1867, will contain the following
New Works :—

*The Seaboard Parish.*
By the Author of "Annals of a
Quiet Neighbourhood."

*Old Testament Characters.*
By THOMAS GUTHRIE, D.D.

*The Religious Life, in Hymns
and Carols and Psalms.*
By the Mistress of a Household.

*Occupations of a Retired Life.*
By EDWARD GARRETT.

*Out of the History of the
Church.*
By Professor ISLAY BURNS.

*Saving Knowledge.*
By THOMAS GUTHRIE, D.D. and
W. G. BLAIKIE, D.D.

The Yearly Volumes of the "Sunday Magazine" are Handsomely Bound in Mauve cloth extra, and Full Gilt, price 8s. 6d. each.

\*.\* *Each Year's Issue forms a Complete Book.*

The Back Volumes and Parts of the "Sunday Magazine" are always in print, and may be had by order of any Bookseller.

On the 1st of each Month, price 2s. 6d.

# The Contemporary Review.

## Theological, Literary, and Social.

The "Contemporary Review" numbers among its Contributors those who, holding loyally to belief in the Articles of the Christian Faith, are not afraid of Modern Thought in its varied aspects and demands, and scorn to defend their faith by mere reticence, or by the artifices too commonly acquiesced in.

The following are among the Contributors to the Numbers already published :—

Alexander, William, D.D. Bishop of Derry.
Alford, Henry, D.D. Dean of Canterbury.
Blakesley, the Rev. Canon.
Bunbury, E. H., M.A.
Cheetham, the Rev. Professor, King's College.
Colquhoun, J. C., M.A.
Davies, the Rev. J. Ll., M.A.
Derner, Dr. J. A., Berlin.
Dowden, Edward.
Fremantle, the Rev. W. H., M.A.
Goodwin, Harvey, D.D., Dean of Ely.
Hannah, the Rev. John, D.C.L.
Humphry, the Rev. W. G., B.D.
Howson, J. S , D.D.
Kinnear, J. Boyd.
Lake, the Rev. W. C., M.A.

Lightfoot, the Rev. Professor, D.D.
Lyttelton, Lord.
Mansel, the Rev. Professor, Oxford.
Merivale, the Rev. Charles, D.C.L.
MacDonnell, John, D.D., Dean of Cashel.
Perowne, Rev. J. J. Stewart, D.D.
Plumptre, the Rev. E. H., M.A.
Reichel, C. P., D.D.
Robertson, the Rev. Canon, M.A.
Shaw, Benjamin, M.A.
Stanley, A. P., D.D., Dean of Westminster.
Stevenson, Rev. W. Fleming.
Tristram, the Rev. H. B., M A.
Tulloch, the Rev. Principal.
Tyrwhitt, the Rev. R. St. John, M.A
Vaughan, the Rev. Edward T., M.A.
Westcott, the Rev. Brooke F., B.D.

The First Five Volumes of the "Contemporary Review" are now ready, bound in cloth, royal 8vo. price 10s. 6d. each. They can be had from any Bookseller, or direct from the Publisher ; and the Monthly Numbers can also be had from the beginning, price 2s. 6d. each.

LONDON : R. CLAY, SON, AND TAYLOR, PRINTERS.